D0208355

EYES *of an* ANGEL

OTHER BOOKS AND BOOKS ON CASSETTE BY DAN YATES:

Angels Don't Knock

Just Call Me an Angel

Angels to the Rescue

An Angel in the Family

It Takes an Angel

An Angel's Christmas

Angel on Vacation

An Angel in Time

EYES *of an* ANGEL

a novel

Dan Yates

Covenant Communications, Inc.

Published by Covenant Communications, Inc.
American Fork, Utah

Printed in Canada
First Printing: August 2002

09 08 07 06 05 04 03 02   10 9 8 7 6 5 4 3 2 1

ISBN 1-59156-083-7

Library of Congress Cataloging -in-Publication Data

Yates, Dan, 1934-
     Eyes of an angel : a novel / Dan Yates
        p. cm.
     ISBN 1-59156-083-7 (alk. paper)
     1. Angels--Fiction. 2. Widowers--Fiction. I. Title.

PS3575.A763 E98 2002
813'.54--dc21

2002073476

CHAPTER 1

To Allison Barker, this most recent assignment was a celestial dream come true. The wonder of working so closely with the man she loved, the man she had to leave behind all those years ago when she walked through the door into her present immortal world, was beyond words. She knew this assignment was temporary and would end as soon as her mission was complete. That was okay. She had made up her mind to enjoy every second of her time with Ivan. He would enjoy it too—she'd see to that. If only she could make him understand she was real and not just a whim of his imagination. On the day she had accepted this assignment two months ago, she was positive making him believe would be a cakewalk. Now, she had to admit this was a mistake in judgement. But Allison wasn't one to let difficulty slow her down, especially when the stakes were as high as they were with this assignment.

She sighed and let her thoughts return back those many years to the time of her first angelic assignment, one centering around her own daughter. That was a difficult first assignment but one Allison felt belonged to her alone. And, as seen through the eyes of an angel, it was an assignment with a rewarding twist. Not so for her loved ones left behind in the mortal world. To them, the effects of the blackened deed that led to Allison's first assignment still lingered like a circling vulture to this very day. That was why so much depended on her succeeding in this assignment. Failure was not an option. Brushing aside a tear, she let her memory return to that night so long ago when it all started.

* * *

Charley Stapleton, Allison's brother, lowered his night-vision goggles and glanced with concern at Detective Ed Quinn, who was crouched next to him behind the fallen log. "What if this guy makes the pickup in a high-speed boat?" Charley asked. "How are you going to stop him?"

The detective spoke without lowering his goggles. "I'm not worried about a boat, Charley. The chopper we have positioned just over the hill could be on him in a matter of seconds. My greatest concern is he might not show at all."

One eyebrow raised as Charley mulled over Quinn's theory. "He's the one who made up the rules for this drop. Why go to all the trouble, then not even grab the money?"

"We're dealing with a shrewd one here, Charley. The guy may be using this little fiasco as a test run. If I'm right, he could set some even harder demands for the next go-around. And the longer this thing drags on, the less chance we have of getting your niece and the boy back alive."

Charley felt a shudder at the suggestion this might drag on beyond tonight. Thoughts of what Rene and Lance must have been going through pained him. "What kind of sicko would hurt a young mother and her child?" he angrily questioned Quinn.

This time the detective did lower his goggles. "Count yourself lucky you don't have my job, Charley. I run into guys almost on a daily basis who'd slit their own mother's throat for the price of a joint."

"Why would the guy pick my niece and her son to kidnap, Detective? Granted, Ivan is wealthy enough to be targeted by some greedy lowlife, but there are thousands of other rich guys out there. Why Rene and Lance?"

"How does a guy like this ever choose his target?" Quinn pondered aloud. "My guess on this one would be because Ivan was in the news recently for prosecuting Blake Campbell. Any time an attorney wins a case against a drug lord like Campbell, it brings publicity. I'm only guessing, but I'd say this is probably what caught the kidnapper's eye."

Charley felt sick. He checked his watch to see it was nearly 2:00 A.M., the time set by the kidnapper for Ivan, Charley's brother-in-law and husband to his beloved sister, Allison, to make the drop. All Charley could do was pray the kidnapper wouldn't suspect he had gone to the police. If the culprit had the slightest hint the place was staked out, it could spell big trouble.

Charley had found the ransom note pinned to his front door yesterday morning. The note had warned him against going to the police and had given specific instructions on how the drop was to be made. Ivan Barker was to place $500,000 in a briefcase and bring it to this remote campsite on the north shore of Roosevelt Lake at exactly 2:00 A.M. There, he was told, he'd find a trash can marked with a wrapping of wide, yellow ribbon. He was to deposit the briefcase into the open can, then get in his car and drive straight home.

The decision to go to Detective Quinn, even though the note warned against it, was one of the most difficult Charley ever had to make. Quinn assured him he had done the right thing and personally took charge of the operation. He immediately had Ivan picked up and transported to headquarters, where Quinn told him the news. Charley was more than a little put out when Ivan refused to listen to Detective Quinn's proposal. Quinn wanted to fill the briefcase with newspaper, explaining that as long as the kidnapper didn't have the money, he'd consider a live hostage to be a bargaining lever. But once the money changed hands, the hostage would become a liability to be disposed of as quickly as possible. Regardless of Quinn's insistence, Ivan refused to listen. To him, no amount of money was worth risking Rene's and Lance's lives, and he was convinced not paying the ransom would put them at greater risk.

"There!" Detective Quinn whispered frantically, yanking Charley from his thoughts. "It's Ivan's Porsche. He's pulling into the campsite now."

The campsite was located at a point about three hundred feet below where Charley and Detective Quinn were crouched. "I see," Charley anxiously responded, checking for himself. "I pray this goes well."

"We're all praying it goes well," the detective returned, never taking his eyes off Ivan. "But more often than not in these cases, things don't go well. Nauseating as it sounds, the kidnapper has the upper hand. He knows exactly where he's headed. Our job is to outguess him, something that's never easy."

Charley watched Ivan's Porsche roll to a stop. The door opened and Ivan stepped out, holding the briefcase of ransom money. He walked straight to the trash can, which was placed only feet from the shoreline. Ivan glanced briefly around, then made the drop. Scurrying back to his car, he climbed in and drove back toward the road. It was decided in advance that he was to drive straight home. Detective Quinn felt this was best, since the kidnapper had specified it and might have an accomplice watching Ivan.

"That went as well as we could expect," Quinn observed as Ivan's car disappeared into the darkness. "Now, we can settle in for the wait. There's no way of knowing how long that may be." Quinn lifted a large, stainless steel thermos from which he refilled a cup of coffee. He glanced over at Charley. "You want some of this, pal? You can use the thermos cap for a cup."

"Come on," Charley replied. "You know I'm a hot chocolate man."

"Suit yourself," Quinn said, laying the thermos back down. "But this could turn into a long night. I need all the help I can get to keep these eyes open."

Charley wasn't one who understood the criminal mind. He just assumed the kidnapper would make his pickup within minutes following the drop. As it turned out, this idea couldn't have been more wrong. Minutes turned into hours, and the hours dragged painfully on until the first rays of daylight broke across the eastern sky. "What do you think, Detective?" Charley wearily asked, realizing even in his untrained mind that a pickup was less likely in daylight.

"I don't know," the detective admitted, the strain showing in his own voice. "I'm afraid our boy isn't going to show."

Suddenly, the early morning stillness was shattered by the deafening report of a gigantic explosion. Charley's eyes shot back to the campsite to see the whole place engulfed in a massive ball of orange flame.

"What the!" Quinn shouted, leaping to his feet. "We've been duped!" Quinn broke for the campsite with Charley not two steps behind. In a painful effort to catch his breath following the brisk run, Charley grabbed his first look at the chaos. What was left of the trash can lay in a crumpled heap more than a hundred feet from its original location. A gaping hole the size of a small house had been ripped open where the shoreline had once lain, and was now rapidly filling with lake water. Quinn smashed the toe of one boot angrily at the ground. "I don't know how this guy did it!" he bellowed. "But he made the pickup right under our noses! Now he has the money and no reason to keep his hostages alive!"

Glancing down at his feet, Charley spotted a still-smoldering bit of yellow ribbon. Bending down, he picked it up and crushed out the last traces of flame between his thumb and forefinger. "What do you have there?" Quinn asked, reaching out to take the ribbon from Charley.

"Just a piece of the yellow ribbon," Charley answered.

"You better let me have it," Quinn instructed. "It's a long shot, but it might offer a clue."

Charley handed it to Quinn, then turned to stare out across the dark waters of Roosevelt Lake. Reflections from the morning sun danced like sparkling diamonds atop ripples created from the blast, but Charley's thoughts weren't on the lake just now. Nor were they on anything as warm as a morning sun. His thoughts were much colder as he wondered if he'd ever see Rene and Lance alive again.

* * *

Allison drew a long breath as these memories played vividly through her mind's eye. Twenty-five years had come and gone since that dreadful night, bringing countless changes to the lives of those she loved so dearly. Throughout those years, she had enjoyed the privilege of being a guardian angel not just to her beloved husband, but also to another pair of loving souls so very close to her heart. This was a calling she didn't take lightly and one she had always given her best. But in spite of it all, she had yet to achieve one major part of her mission that had always remained at arm's length. With time and events rapidly culminating to the climax she knew was imminent, the urgency of fulfilling her mission was paramount in her mind. For that reason she had approached the authorities with a desperate request: let her appear to Ivan as more than an invisible guardian angel. She knew what she was asking was something seldom approved, but she argued it would only be until she could reach Ivan with her message. After that, she would ask nothing more.

When the authorities answered with a "yes," Alison was overcome with immense joy and a mountain of relief. But if she thought this new arrangement would make short work of her mission, she quickly learned otherwise the first time she appeared to Ivan. She carefully picked what she thought was the best time and place—the breakfast table in the privacy of his own home. She had assumed he would be thrilled at seeing her, but instead he was scared half out of his wits. That hurt—having the man she loved bolt away in fear. Even after he regained his wits, all he could say was he must be losing his mind. There she was, a real angel with a real message, and all Ivan could think was he was losing his mind.

That was two months ago, and Allison had been giving it her best effort ever since. She was making headway. At least he wasn't afraid of her anymore. In fact, he even seemed to enjoy her visits. The problem was, she knew time was growing short. If she didn't complete her mission very soon, the consequences would be inevitable. She couldn't let herself think such thoughts. Today would be the day she convinced him to believe.

CHAPTER 2

Being a successful lawyer meant good days and bad days for Ivan Barker when it came to courtroom showdowns. Today was a good day—of a sort. At least he had managed to add one more notch to his already-long string of legal victories. But, as so often was the case in a courtroom battle, this victory was hollow. Obtaining conviction for a drunken driver who had deprived a young mother of her husband in a high-speed smash-up wasn't all that thrilling when Ivan considered the guilty driver was only a boy himself—nineteen years old and facing a prison term that would put him in his forties before his next breath as a free man. The one Ivan would really have liked to see behind bars was the person who sold this boy the liquor in the first place.

Ivan shoved a stack of papers back in his briefcase and headed for the courtroom door, hoping to avoid people on his way out. He wasn't in the mood for conversation right now. Certain things about this case hit a little too close to home to suit Ivan. It stirred too many old memories of his own daughter, Rene, who became a single mother when she lost her husband in a horrific accident. Another case of no winners. Only with Rene, it wasn't a liquor salesman's guilt—it was Ivan's. A guilt so compelling it had haunted him every day of his life since.

Once out of the building, Ivan made his way to the parking garage where his Lexus awaited. Approaching the car, he pressed the remote on his key ring—shutting off the alarm and simultaneously unlocking the doors. For years Ivan had carried a little trinket on his key ring, one containing an encapsulated bit of yellow ribbon. Every time he looked at the trinket, it reminded him of one dreadful night a quarter-century ago.

Ivan had noticed the trinket on his friend Ed Quinn's desk when he was in Ed's office representing a client some years back. Ed had previously had the bit of ribbon encapsulated as a reminder of a kidnapping case he had completely bungled—Rene's kidnapping. When Ivan learned the origin of the tape, he asked Quinn if he might have it. Quinn obliged, and Ivan had carried it ever since. It became a symbol of his grief, and more pointedly—his guilt.

Ivan slid behind the wheel and pulled the Lexus out of the garage. It was early enough in the afternoon he could have returned to the pile of work waiting in his office, but he just didn't want to. For some reason, he had a compelling urge to drive by the old house on Dana Avenue. It had been years since he last saw the place, and he just felt like seeing it now. It was only a short drive, one that took him less than ten minutes.

The house still looked nice. It was older, of course, but had a certain "lived in" look which spoke of a tenant who obviously cared about the place. It seemed small by the standards of Ivan's home today, much smaller than it had seemed the day Ivan carried his beautiful bride across the threshold. Back then it almost felt like Cinderella's castle, right down to the steep, wooden-shingled roof and pixylike windows. It was blue in those days. Not that the place didn't look nice the way it was now. The pale green seemed to blend well with a landscape that had naturally matured over the years.

Those first ten years living there with Allison were the happiest of Ivan's life. But his happiness turned bitter the last year they spent together. If God wanted to take one of them, why couldn't He have chosen Ivan and spared Allison? But that wasn't to be. All Ivan could do was stand by and watch helplessly while the woman he loved wasted away from the ravages of breast cancer. Undoubtedly the cruelest blow of all came with the realization she could have been saved if only the cancer had been detected in time.

Ivan remembered wondering why it always seemed to rain at funerals. Watching Allison's casket being lowered into the cold, wet ground was the most difficult thing he ever had to endure. If it hadn't been for Rene, he might have simply given up. But little ten-year-old Rene needed him to be strong, so he bit the bullet and willed himself to go on.

Was it really such a bad thing for Ivan to want Rene to pursue a career in medicine? As an oncologist she might have helped other women, maybe even saving some from the same disease that took her mother's life. To Ivan this was a lofty goal, and one he just assumed Rene wanted as badly for herself as he wanted it for her. If only he'd taken the time to listen. Maybe then things would have worked out differently. But it was history now, and there wasn't one thing he could do to change a single second of it.

Ivan circled the block and drove slowly past the old house again. As he did, he noticed a familiar figure had suddenly appeared in the seat next to him. Even though he knew Allison was only there in the folds of his own imagination, he welcomed her company anyway. "I was wondering if you might show up," he said to her. "I mean, with my reminiscing about you and all."

"I noticed we were having a bit of a pity party," Allison remarked. "So, what sort of thoughts are running through that melancholy mind about now?"

This apparition had first visited Ivan a couple of months back, just as he was about to bite into a slice of bacon. His entire plate ended up on the kitchen floor. All his life Ivan had dealt with stress in a sensible and logical way, and suddenly his mind had just snapped. Right there, in the middle of his kitchen, stood the imagined ghost of his long-departed wife. The strangest thing of all was Ivan didn't realize he was even under any added stress. Once the initial shock passed, he had to admit there was a certain amount of pleasantry in seeing this extremely vivid image of his wife. She was so beautiful, and the warmth of her smile reached every corner of his heart. If he had to have a mental breakdown, he couldn't have picked a better way to do it.

To his complete amazement, the apparition was so realistic she even began conversing with him. It was almost a logical conversation, all except the part where she told him she was there with some sort of message he needed to hear. That was carrying things just a little too far, so this part he did his best to screen out.

That day in his kitchen was only the beginning. There hadn't been a day since that he hadn't imagined her with him at least once. At first he considered counseling but quickly rejected the idea.

Imagined or not, there was no denying how much he enjoyed these little visits. Why pay some psychologist to make her go away? What possible harm could come from playing this little game, just as long as no one else ever found out?

"I was thinking about us," Ivan responded to Allison's question about his thoughts. "Back when the real you was here with me, I mean. I'm still in love with you, you know."

She smiled. "And I love you, Ivan. That's the way it's supposed to be when two people promise themselves to each other forever."

"Forever?" Ivan sighed. "Somehow forever seems so very far away right now."

"It's much closer than you think. And the best part is, our forever includes more than just you and me, Ivan. You seem to have lost sight of that right now, but it is true."

Allison's words brought an icy pain to Ivan's heart. "Meaning Rene," he remarked. It wasn't a question, but a statement void of emotion.

"Yes, Rene," Allison firmly stated. "And Lance. And let's not forget Neil. They're all part of our forever family, Ivan."

"Stop it!" Ivan suddenly shouted as the pain welled up inside. "After what I did to Rene, she could never forgive me. As for Lance, well he doesn't even know he has a grandfather. And Neil is another story altogether. There's no use even going there."

Allison shook her head. "You're wrong, Ivan. And do you know why you're wrong? Because you're overlooking one of the greatest of all human attributes, the ability to forgive. When I say forgive, I mean the word in its fullest sense—which includes forgiving oneself. In the case of our family, that's the only piece of the puzzle still missing, you forgiving yourself. Only you can put the final piece into the puzzle, and when you do, the picture of our forever family will be complete. And that, Ivan Barker, is the very reason I'm here. To bring you to the point where you can forgive yourself."

Ivan gripped the wheel with a firmness that turned his knuckles white. "I'm in no frame of mind to handle talking about these things today, Allison. If you insist on hanging around to haunt me, can you at least change the subject?"

Ivan glanced quickly over at her, hoping his sharp tongue hadn't driven her away. To his relief, she was still there. "All right, Ivan," she calmly agreed. "We won't talk about Rene. Let's talk about Jamie instead."

Ivan rolled his eyes. "You never knew Jamie," he refuted. "Why do you keep pretending you know her?"

"There's no pretending to it! I've been right there beside you every step of the way with Jamie. And that brings up another point. You can just add Jamie's name to the list we've already discussed for our forever family. Whether you know it or not, she's every bit as much my daughter as she is yours. I wish you'd get that through your head."

Ivan thought how wonderful it would be if the things this imagined ghost was saying were really true. What would he give to believe himself still worthy of belonging to such a forever family? But he had long ago given up that right with mistakes that could never be erased. Mistakes that had tormented him for more than half a lifetime. And regardless of what this imagined ghost said, the real Allison had never known Jamie. She couldn't have. Jamie was born fourteen years after Allison's death.

The first time Ivan saw Jamie, she was nine and had just gone through the appalling experience of losing both parents to a senseless act of violence. There were no living relatives, and the court was trying to decide what to do with the child. To this day Ivan couldn't say what caused the bond he and Jamie instantly felt for each other. Whatever the cause, the bond was definitely real. Maybe his part of it had something to do with his prior failure as a father. He couldn't say for sure, but this theory did make sense. Jamie was ten by the time Ivan convinced the court he could make a suitable, single father. Ironically, ten was the same age Rene had been when Allison died and Ivan set out on his own to raise her. The day Jamie walked into Ivan's house as his legal daughter was the day the house came alive again.

Ivan glanced back at Allison. "I wish you could have known Jamie," he said. "You would have loved her. She's like Rene in so many ways. She's grown up to be a beautiful young woman. She's engaged, you know. To a nice young man named Milton Taylor. She and Milton work together at his private detective agency."

"I know all of this," Allison affirmed. "But how can you call Milton Taylor a young man? He's thirteen years Jamie's senior. And he's no more the right man for her than Robert Cranston was right for Rene. You were blind back then, Ivan Barker. And from what you're saying, it sounds like you're just as blind now."

"You have to throw Robert Cranston in my face, don't you?" Ivan grumbled. "I admit I was wrong about him, but I am not wrong about Milton. This time it's not just my idea. Jamie accepted Milton's ring on her own."

"She may have accepted his ring, but you'll notice she hasn't set a date to marry him. And do you know why? Because subconsciously she knows Milton's not the right one, that's why."

"Okay, so if he's not the right one, then who is?"

A teasing smile crossed Allison's lips. "Don't think I don't know the answer to that, Ivan. I'm just not permitted to tell you yet."

By now Ivan had made another circle around the block and was passing the old house a third time. After taking one last look, he shoved his foot down on the accelerator. "I'm going home now, Allison," he stated, ignoring her last remark. "I need to change into something more casual since Jamie invited me to dinner at her apartment tonight." Ivan glanced over at Allison and winked. "I have an idea," he proposed. "You're always going on about how I don't believe you're real. Come along with me tonight and show yourself to Jamie. Can you think of a better way to prove yourself?" Ivan knew his proposal was laughable, but he just wanted to see Allison's reaction.

"I'm not permitted to show myself to anyone else, Ivan. I've told you that. I don't know what I'm going to do with you if you don't stop pushing me away like this. I am real, I am here, and I do love you."

"Fine. Then you can at least hang around long enough to help me pick out something suitable to wear tonight. You know how Jamie teases me when I wear something that doesn't match."

Ivan's cell phone rang before Allison could respond. Pulling to a stop next to the curb, he removed the phone from his belt and glanced at the caller ID. *Unknown Caller.* He wasn't in the mood for a telemarketer, if that's what this call was. But he couldn't afford not to answer it, since it was quite possibly a client. He glanced over at Allison just as the phone rang for the fourth time. "You want to convince me you're real?" he said. "Here's another chance. Tell me who's on the other end of this call."

Allison responded with an annoyed shrug. "I'm not a mind reader, dear. And I don't hold supernatural powers that allow me to foretell things like phone calls. How many times must I tell you?"

Ivan grinned, completely amused by her predictable response, and pressed the receive button on his phone. "Hello, Ivan Barker here."

CHAPTER 3

As they waited for the light to turn green, Charley glanced over at the young man driving the car. Was it possible this was the five-year-old boy Charley had taken to raise when Rene met her untimely death? He felt a swelling of pride in his chest as he contemplated what a fine young man Lance had grown into. He wished he could take credit, but knowing the sort of makeshift father he'd been over the years pretty much extinguished that idea. He reasoned the real credit went to the five years Rene had with Lance and to Lance himself. He was just the kind of individual who could absorb whatever blow life might throw his way and still remain on his feet.

The light turned green, and Lance drove the remaining half block to the address where the letter had indicated the lab would be. Pulling into the parking lot, he chose a spot near the front of the building. From the outside it looked like any other office building, maybe housing a dental office or brokerage firm. But it was what Charley knew waited inside that made it so special.

The two of them left the car and headed straight for the entrance. There, they paused to read the words stenciled on the door. *FORENSIC CRIMINAL SCIENCE LAB*. "I can't believe this is really happening, Uncle Charley," Lance exclaimed excitedly. "I have my very own forensic lab! And I'm about to turn a lifetime dream into reality!"

Charley moved to the door, shoved a key in the lock, and gave the knob a twist. Then, stepping aside, he allowed Lance the first look inside. "I've died and gone to heaven," Lance cried with glee. "Look at all this stuff, Uncle Charley." Lance stepped through the door and

Charley was just about to follow when a movement at the corner of the building caught his eye. He turned just in time to catch one glimpse of a man in a trench coat and wide-brimmed hat disappear around the building. *What strange attire for someone to wear in the Arizona desert,* Charley thought as an eerie feeling crept over him. Had this man been watching them? He quickly shook it off as a dumb idea and stepped inside the lab. Just as he had supposed, it looked exactly as it had in the picture. He smiled at Lance, who had his eye pressed to the lens of an electronic microscope.

"Just look at this stuff, Charley!" Lance cried out again, stepping back to take in the scene of the whole lab. "This is unbelievable!"

"What did you expect, kid?" Charley answered calmly. "That's what the letter said it would be."

Charley did a quick inventory on his own. Even with his limited knowledge of this sort of thing, he was certain all the equipment Lance would ever need was here. Charley couldn't even venture a guess as to how much all this cost. Whoever the mysterious benefactor was, he certainly wasn't cutting any corners. But then, he never had been one to cut corners.

The anonymous benefactor and his gifts had first shown up when a letter arrived in Charley's mailbox on the very day Lance was to graduate from high school. The letter arrived containing two items: a bank draft for $10,000 and instructions for how the money was to be used. The $10,000 was for the initial expense of setting up Lance's education in criminal forensic science, something Lance had dreamed of studying all his young life but had no realistic way of financing on his own. The letter went on to explain that Lance had been enrolled by proxy at the University of Central Florida in Orlando. More money was promised to follow as it was needed.

Charley would never forget Lance's reaction when he told him about the letter. *Yeah, right, some anonymous benefactor wants to send me to school? Get real, Uncle Charley. I know what a practical joker you can be, but you're carrying this a little far.* It took some doing on Charley's part to convince Lance the check was real, but somehow he managed. That letter changed the course of Lance's life. The benefactor saw to it that his every educational need was taken care of. Whenever the perpetual account ran low, it would be shored up by a mysterious deposit. Only when Lance had his diploma in hand did the money stop.

After college Lance chose to remain in Florida. He applied for and was readily accepted as a forensic investigator in the homicide division of the Orlando Police Department. He'd been with them four years now. As for the benefactor—neither Lance nor Charley expected to ever hear from him again. But they were wrong.

Charley had recently gone to Hollywood, where he found work filming an Energizer Battery commercial. He had just returned home to his apartment when he discovered this latest letter waiting. He was alone in the apartment when he read the letter, but his elated shouts caught the attention of several tenants, who came running. Embarrassed as he was, he just couldn't help it. The excitement of what he had read was too overwhelming. He did some fast talking to get them all calmed down, then made a quick call to Lance.

* * *

"Guess what just happened, kid!" he shouted into the phone.

Lance responded with a laugh. "What's got you so excited, Charley?"

"I just got another letter from your anonymous benefactor! You'll never believe what this guy's been up to the whole time!"

"Another letter? Slow down, Charley, and fill me in. What about this letter?"

"I know why he paid for your education!" Charley anxiously stated. "He wants you to reopen your mother's unsolved murder case."

"He what?!" Lance echoed with a shout of his own. "How am I supposed to do that?"

"He's leased you a forensic lab in Mesa, kid. Back where you lived when your mom was murdered. He sent me a picture of it and the keys to the door. He assures me the lab is equipped with all the latest stuff you'll need to reopen the case."

"A forensic lab? In Mesa? Are you kidding, Charley?"

"It's the truth, kid, so help me! And the best part is, the benefactor says the lab is yours as long as you need it. He wants you to get started as soon as possible. Can you break away from your job okay?"

There was only a brief pause. "Yeah, I'm sure I can get a leave of absence. It'll take me a day or two to put everything in order here, but I'm sure I can arrange everything."

"Okay, kid. What about this? I'll finish up my business here in Hollywood and meet you at Phoenix Sky Harbor airport one week from today. Does that give you enough time?"

"I'm sure it's enough time, Charley. Oh, my gosh! Am I dreaming or what?"

"There's one more thing the benefactor added in the letter. There's a young woman living in Mesa who he'll have contact you. She knows her way around the place and can give you a big hand in that way."

"A young woman?" Lance asked in a calmer voice. "What's her name?"

"Don't know. The guy didn't give me a name. He just said she'd look you up."

"That's odd," Lance observed.

"No odder than the way your benefactor keeps himself hidden, kid. He must have some reason for working that way. So, we'll meet in one week, is that the plan?"

* * *

The meeting at the airport had taken place just over an hour ago. The two of them had grabbed a bite to eat, rented a car, and headed straight to the lab. Charley's thoughts were interrupted when Lance suddenly grabbed his hand and jabbed it with a needlelike instrument. "Ow!" Charley fussed. "That hurt! What are you doing?"

"I needed a sample of your blood," Lance excitedly explained. "I want to show you something that'll amaze you." Lance moved to a lab table containing a computer and several other pieces of complicated-looking equipment that Charley couldn't name. There, he prepared a slide containing the sample of Charley's blood. Next he drew a sample of his own blood and added it to the slide. Inserting the slide in the electronic microscope, he placed his eye to the lens and adjusted the focus. As Charley looked on in astonishment, Lance punched in a few commands on the computer, bringing two sets of squiggle lines to the screen—all of which meant nothing to Charley.

"Look!" Lance exclaimed, pointing to the upper trace. "That's you, Uncle Charley. And this lower trace is me. Now watch what happens when I overlay the two traces."

Charley leaned a little closer as he watched the two traces merge into one. "You see that, Uncle Charley!" Lance cried. "This is positive proof you and I are closely related. Just look at how close our two blood samples match up. If you ever questioned whether you were my mother's real uncle, this should put all doubt to rest."

Charley shook his head. "Why would I ever question Rene was my niece?" he puzzled.

"Well, you know, just in case. This proves it beyond all doubt. Doesn't that excite you at all?"

"Oh, yeah, it excites me. It's always nice to have a computer tell me something I've known all my life."

Lance's mood suddenly shifted to be more serious. "I just don't get it, Charley," he remarked, slowly shaking his head. "Why is this benefactor interested enough in my mother to provide me with this expensive lab? Who could this man be?" Lance thought a moment, then added, "I guess we're not really sure he's even a man. It's possible she's a woman. We don't even know that much."

Charley considered this. Lance was right, there really wasn't any way of saying for sure the benefactor was a man, even though Charley had always pictured a man. "Believe me, kid, I wish I could answer your questions. But the fact is, I haven't a clue. The guy—or gal, as the case may be—has yet to do one thing to tip us off as to who they are. Both letters came with no return address, and the postmarks were Canadian."

"Yeah," Lance answered. "The Canada thing was probably used to throw us off."

Charley shrugged. "This person obviously likes working from the shadows and wants to keep things that way. But never look a gift horse in the mouth, I always say."

"You're probably right," Lance agreed. "I'm sure our anonymous friend knows what he or she is doing. But I wonder how long I'll have to wait before this lady mentioned in the letter looks me up."

"I'm guessing it won't be long," Charley surmised. "Like I said, our benefactor friend always has things pretty much in hand."

"Hey!" Lance suddenly shouted. "I have an idea! Do you have the letter with you?"

Charley shot an inquisitive look at Lance. "The letter from the benefactor?" he asked.

"Yeah. Do you have it with you?"

Charley pulled out an envelope from his inside blazer pocket and handed it to Lance. "So, what's this idea that has you so excited?" he quizzed.

Lance took the envelope and removed the letter, which he unfolded and placed face down on a scanner that sat next to the computer. Next he grabbed a blank sheet of paper from a sticky pad and handed it to Charley. "Press your fingers down on this," he instructed. "I need a sample of your prints."

Charley obliged and Lance placed the pad alongside the letter in the scanner, pulling the information into the computer. "Take a look at this, Charley," he said, pointing to the screen. "The letter is covered with fingerprints. The way I see it, some of them are yours . . ."

"And some of them are the benefactor's!" Charley shouted, suddenly understanding where Lance was going.

"That's right, provided the benefactor didn't wipe the letter clean before sealing it. Watch this." Lance entered a computer command, and most of the fingerprints on the letter suddenly vanished.

Charley's eyes shot open. "What did you do, kid? Where did those prints go?"

"Simple, Charley. I took a sample of your print and told the computer to erase everything that matched. The remainder of the prints definitely belong to someone else. I'm guessing that someone is our benefactor."

Charley laid a finger on the screen, as if feeling the prints would make them more real. "Do you know what this means?" he grinned.

"Yes, my happy little uncle, I do know what it means. It means we're one step closer to putting a name to the person. I'll save these prints to a file. Who knows what may come of it down the road?"

"An exciting thought," Charley agreed.

Lance nodded. "Yes, but not as exciting as the thought of reopening the case of my mother's murder. Do you have any idea what this means to me, Uncle Charley?"

Charley blew out a long breath. "I think I do, kid. About as much as it means to me. Nothing would do my heart more good than to see that madman brought to justice. I was there when he made off with the ransom money right under our noses. I've never forgiven myself. There must have been something more I could have done than sit there waiting for the dawn to break, then watch all the evidence go up in a puff of smoke."

"No, Uncle Charley," Lance assured. "It wasn't your fault. There wasn't anything you or anyone else could have done with the information you had at the time. The killer had the upper hand, and he took full advantage of it."

"That's easy for you to say, kid. But I was there. Thanks to your grandfather, your poor mother had it rough enough without having to leave this old world the way she did. If there's one thing I don't feel bad about, it's him losing all that ransom money. I've often wondered if that didn't hurt him more than losing his daughter."

"You shouldn't say that, Uncle Charley. You don't know what was in my grandfather's heart. I know the story of how it supposedly happened, since you've told it to me often enough. But I've never completely felt like my grandfather was as guilty as you've made him out to be."

Charley closed his eyes in thought. "You didn't know him, kid. And you didn't know your own daddy. Your mother loved your daddy as much as any woman can love any man. Your granddaddy had no right to keep those two apart. If he'd left well enough alone, you might have been raised by a mother and father instead of a near-worthless uncle once-removed."

Lance chuckled. "How can you say that about yourself, Uncle Charley? You loved me, and love is the most important thing you could have given me."

"I loved you, I'll give you that. Still do, kid. I loved your momma too. When she asked me to raise you if anything ever happened to her, I didn't bat an eye. I knew how badly she wanted you kept away from your granddaddy. But you growing up with an uncle looking for work wherever he could find it wasn't the best thing that could have happened."

"Hey, I didn't mind. It was sort of neat, being raised by a real movie star."

"Movie star? Yeah, right! I was lucky to get whatever part I could in a movie, television production, stage production—who cared. Work was work, but I never knew where I'd have to go to find it, and you ended up tagging along through a lot of moves. The worst part was dragging you from school to school the way I had to do."

"It didn't hurt me, Uncle Charley. They taught the same subjects in all the schools I attended, and look at all the friends I made along the way."

"Thanks, kid. I did the best I knew how raising you, and even if you don't always mean it, I love hearing you say it." Charley glanced at his watch. "I hope you don't mind if I leave you to all your new playthings while I go meet with some old acquaintances in this town. With any luck, I might land some kind of job while we're here."

"No problem, Uncle Charley. Like you say, I have plenty to keep me busy. Take the car, I want to spend most of the day here in the lab. I'll catch a taxi to the motel later this evening."

Charley stepped from the building and drew in a breath, filling his lungs with fresh desert air and his mind with nostalgic memories of his boyhood growing up in this town. So engrossed was he in his own thoughts that he failed to notice the shadowy figure of a man half-hidden by the dense shrubbery landscaping the grounds. A man whose eyes followed Charley's every move.

* * *

Once Lance was alone in his new lab, he set to work saving the benefactor's fingerprints to a file. As he did, he made a startling discovery. Some of the prints showed signs of skin damage, such as might be expected from exposure to a serious fire. One more little bit of information about his anonymous benefactor. Lance had to laugh. Here he was using the very equipment his anonymous benefactor had provided in an effort to unmask him—or her.

Once the file was prepared, Lance leaned back on his lab stool and contemplated more about this lady the benefactor said would contact him. He couldn't help wondering who she might be and what she might be like. There was little he could do but wait, and he found himself hoping the wait wouldn't be too long. He glanced around the room at all the new toys at his disposal. One thing he knew for sure, he wouldn't get bored while he waited. Not with all this new stuff to try out.

CHAPTER 4

Jamie Barker stepped up to the office door marked *Taylor and Barker Detective Agency*. What a thrill to see her own name on the door that for so many years had read simply *Milton Taylor Detective Agency*. Without question, her life had changed for the better because of Milton. He was one of two men she could make that statement about. The other was her own wonderful daddy, Ivan Barker. Ivan didn't have to be her dad; he chose to be her dad. He waged a relentless uphill court battle to make it happen, and he did it at a time when her candle of hope was burning very dimly.

Jamie strongly suspected there was more to her meeting Milton than mere chance. Not that her dad would admit it, of course, but she was almost positive he had a big hand in it. If she was right, it would be out of character for her dad, who almost never interfered in her social life. In fact, he made such a point of staying out of her social life, it almost seemed like an obsession with him. This was another of a fairly long string of observations Jamie had made of her father that she could only chalk up to being the result of something that happened to him before she became a part of his life. For some reason she never quite understood, Ivan refused to talk about his earlier life. From her viewpoint, he didn't have a past but had simply burst into existence in time to become her adopted father.

Jamie did know her dad had married his childhood sweetheart, Allison Stapleton, and that Allison had died eleven years after they were married. This she discovered from Melba Ross, an old friend of Ivan's he had hired to help with Jamie when he had to be away at the office for long periods of time. Jamie knew bits and pieces about her father's past, but she respected his wishes to leave it alone. Someday, she told herself, she'd tackle the job of removing the cloak that kept his yesterdays so completely hidden. Someday, but not just yet.

Jamie pushed open the door and walked into the office, where she spotted Milton working at his desk. He glanced up. "Hi, beautiful," he said, rising from his chair and crossing the room to greet her with an affectionate kiss. "Did you miss me while I was out chasing crooks all over the world?"

Milton had just returned from Paris, France, where he had gone following a hot tip about a murder suspect he'd been tracking the past couple of years. "What do you mean 'did I miss you'?" Jamie joked. "Have you been gone?"

"Only six weeks," he countered before kissing her again.

"So, how did it go?" Jamie asked, playing with a button on his shirt. "Did you bring the culprit to justice or was it a dead end?"

"Caught him flat-footed and bagged him before he knew what hit. He's in a Paris jail waiting extradition back to the States. They don't send Milton Taylor on a job unless they want the job done. Heck, I'm probably better than Deputy Dawg."

Jamie laughed. "Just don't expect me to start ironing your Superman suits if it comes to that."

Milton took both of her hands in his own and looked her straight in the eye. "Did you miss me enough to finally set that date?" he asked.

The question came as no surprise to Jamie, though it did come with a degree of reserve. It wasn't without feelings of guilt that she continued putting off setting a marriage date. Milton was a wonderful man, and she was sure marrying him was the right thing to do. It was just—well, it wasn't something she could actually put her finger on—but she just couldn't bring herself to say exactly when she'd be ready. "I just need a little more time," she pleaded, trying to sound as upbeat as possible. "But I am ready for that lunch you promised over the phone. I'm starved."

Milton's flight was scheduled to arrive in the wee hours of the morning, and he didn't want Jamie meeting him at the airport at such an inconvenient time. In a call before his flight left Paris, he suggested they meet at the office around noon and go for lunch. "I'm a little hungry, too," he admitted. "What sounds good? Chinese? Mexican?"

"Mexican," she quickly noted. "Let's eat at Matta's. I love their Robert's tacos."

"Mexican it is, mi dama hermosa," Milton responded with a smile.

"What?" Jamie laughed.

"I just said Mexican it is, my beautiful lady. But I was just finishing my report on the Paris caper. Can your stomach hold out another five minutes?"

Jamie pushed a finger to the tip of Milton's nose. "Five minutes, okay. Six, and you'll have yourself one irate fiancée."

"Five minutes. It's a promise." He grinned, giving her another quick kiss before returning to his computer.

Jamie moved to her own desk, where she checked her e-mail. Nothing important. She glanced over and watched Milton as he worked. He looked the part of a private detective, from his square-cut jaw right down to those broad shoulders atop his six-foot-two frame. She let her mind drift back to the first time she saw him. It was in a courtroom where Ivan was representing the Brad Johnson Construction Company. Benny Peterson, one of their employees, was suing for permanent disability. Ivan had invited Jamie to meet him in court that morning so they could go for lunch afterward. She entered the courtroom just as Milton was being sworn in as a witness against the plaintiff. Ivan had obtained Milton's services to keep tabs on Benny. In his testimony, Milton produced videos of Benny at a bowling alley, reroofing his covered patio, and riding a motorcycle in an off-road race. The case was thrown out.

Afterward, Ivan asked Milton if he'd like to join them for lunch. Whether it was a spur-of-the-moment arrangement or one prearranged in her dad's mind, Jamie could only guess. She and Milton hit it off right away. She had always been interested in criminology, and finding someone like Milton to discuss it with was exciting. Things turned even more exciting when Milton suggested that Jamie give up her job as a bank teller and come to work for him at his agency. He offered to show her the ropes and even pay her tuition for some criminology courses at the local college. His offer was like a dream come true. Jamie snatched it up, even though it meant a fairly significant pay cut from her bank job. For the first three and a half years, she worked as Milton's assistant during the day and attended college at night. It didn't take long before both she and Milton realized she was a natural.

No one could have been more surprised than Jamie at what happened on her twenty-sixth birthday. Milton threw a surprise party where he presented her with two special gifts. The first was a gorgeous engagement ring, which Jamie accepted on the condition that she didn't have to give him a specific date—a condition Milton graciously agreed to.

It was Milton's second gift that caught Jamie by greater surprise. Without so much as a hint of warning, he made an astounding announcement. He was moving her up to be a partner in the agency. Jamie was at a loss for words, but she made up for it by planting a kiss on Milton's lips—right there for all the world to see. She never knew if the applause came because of her promotion or because of that kiss. She breathed a sigh, realizing that had been eight months ago this very week.

Milton hit the save key on his computer and glanced at his watch. "Four minutes and thirty-nine seconds," he quipped. "Looks like I made the deadline. Let's eat."

"If you're looking for an argument," Jamie said, "you've approached the wrong woman. Let's go."

Milton opened the door for her and remarked, "Who knows, on a full stomach, maybe you'll give that big date some more thought."

Jamie rolled her eyes. "We'll see. But keep an eye on me, will you? Don't let me overeat. I need to leave room for tonight."

They stepped through the door and Milton locked it. "What's happening tonight?" he asked.

"I'm having my dad over for dinner, and I want everything to be perfect—including my own appetite. I've got to prove I can cook a decent meal, and that I'm not starving since moving out. You know how Dad worries."

"Okay," Milton jested. "You get one taco and a glass of water."

"Hey!" she said, slipping an arm through his as they walked toward her car. "You don't have to keep *that* close an eye on me."

* * *

The phone in Ivan's hand rang for the fifth time. He had to laugh at himself for ever thinking Allison's imaginary ghost might tell him who was on the other end. He pressed the receive button. "Hello, Ivan Barker here."

"Ivan Barker, the lawyer, right?" came a gruff male voice in response.

"Yes, that's right."

"You're the one representing Samuel Wagner in the Swineheart murder case?"

"Who is this?" Ivan pressed.

"Just answer my question! Are you the one representing Wagner?"

"I'm representing Samuel Wagner, yes. You want to tell me what this is about?"

"What it's about, Barker, is Wagner's present dilemma. He's got big problems at the moment, pal, and he needs his lawyer in a big way."

Ivan had been working this case for the past few weeks. Wagner was accused of murdering a gangster named Billy Ray Swineheart, but Ivan was convinced he was innocent. Bail had been set at $50,000, which Samuel had little trouble raising. "I'm confused by this," Ivan retorted. "What do you mean Wagner's in trouble?"

"Look," the caller blatantly shot back. "I'm stretching my neck out telling you this much. Just take my word for it, Wagner is in a bind. If you're any kind of lawyer, you'll get over there right now!"

Ivan heard the phone go dead as the caller abruptly ended the conversation. "What was that all about?" Allison asked.

"You're still here?" Ivan remarked with a glance in her direction. "I figured my mind would send you walking with a weird call like this to ponder."

"What was the call about?" Allison pressed. "For some reason, I get this cold feeling it wasn't good."

"It's about nothing we need to discuss," Ivan said, pulling the car back onto the street and heading for Samuel Wagner's house.

"Stop this, Ivan!" Allison insisted. "Tell me what that call was about this instant!"

Ivan turned left at the next corner. "I don't know what it was about. The caller didn't identify himself. He told me I need to get to Samuel Wagner's house because the man's in some sort of trouble."

"Samuel Wagner?" Allison quizzed worriedly. "Isn't he the client who has connections with organized crime?"

"He's not connected with organized crime. He's accused of killing a kingpin who is associated with organized crime. Big difference. Those dirtbags are framing him."

"He has to have some connection with them, Ivan. Even if he is innocent, why else would they try to frame him for murder?"

"I don't have all the answers, Allison. But I've handled enough murder cases in my time to know this one is a frame-up. The evidence against Samuel is too pat. The body was found in the trunk of his car with the murder weapon lying next to it. And the murder weapon was a gun owned by Samuel's ex-wife, a gun she reported stolen a week before the murder. Now I ask you, would Wagner kill someone with a gun that could so readily be traced back to him, put the body in his own car, and leave the gun right there with it? I don't think so. And, on top of all this, some nameless tipster just happens to call the authorities about the body being in Samuel's car? This is a frame from the get-go, Allison, and I'm just the one who can prove it."

Allison was silent a few seconds. "Don't go over to that house!" she at last stated with definite alarm in her voice. "I have a bad feeling about this."

Ivan shifted his eyes to look at her. "I don't see I have any choice. Samuel is my client. If he needs me, I have to be there for him."

"Call the police," Allison countered. "If there's a problem, they're the ones to handle it."

"The police already believe my client is a murderer. I'm not about to add more fuel to the fire. I'll check this out myself."

"Then at least give me Samuel's address, and let me grab an advance look at what you're walking into."

"I can't remember the exact address, Allison. All I know is it's on Birchwood Avenue just east of Gilbert Road. I can find it easy enough since I was there when the police went in with the search warrant following Wagner's arrest."

Allison grew silent again and remained that way until they pulled into the driveway of Samuel's house. "Is this the place?" she asked.

Ivan opened his door and stepped out of the car. "This is it," he replied.

"Then I'm going to have a look inside," she stated, sliding through the unopened door on the passenger's side in the same manner she always moved through closed doors. Ivan hated this and wished he at least had control over this part of his imagined ghost. He watched as she scurried on ahead and passed right through the closed door of the house. Ivan walked to the porch and rang the bell. Seconds later, Allison was back. "Call the police!" she shouted at him. "There's a dead body inside!"

* * *

"Thanks for lunch," Jamie told Milton as she brought the Honda to a stop in front of their detective agency. "Those Robert's tacos hit the spot every time."

Milton opened his door and stepped out. Turning, he leaned in the open window. "Sorry I wasn't better company. It usually takes me a day or so to get the jet lag out of my system."

"Maybe you should go home and get some sleep. There's nothing waiting in the office that won't keep till morning."

Milton stifled a yawn. "I wish that were true. But after being out of the office for the past two weeks, I've got a ton of digging out to do before I can even prioritize what I want to start on next. Good luck with your dinner tonight. Hope it comes off like you want."

Jamie laughed. "Me too."

Milton backed away a step. "I'm sure you'll do great. I'll call you in the morning for the full report." He blew her a kiss, then entered the building.

Jamie glanced in her mirror to be sure it was clear, then pulled out onto the road. She had been planning this dinner long enough to have everything she needed stocked and ready to go—or so she thought, until making one last check of her cupboard before leaving the house this morning. She owned only one set of salt and pepper shakers, and she found the pepper shaker nearly empty, with none in storage to replenish it. *What a mistake it would be not to have any, with the way Dad always piles his food with pepper,* Jamie thought. *No real problem, it just means a stop by the grocery store on the way home.*

* * *

Ivan stared disbelievingly at Allison. "How can my imagination tell me there's a body inside? This is preposterous." He rang the bell again.

"Listen to me!" Allison shouted. "There is a body inside! Get away from here this instant and call the police! You're a lawyer, you know what might happen if you don't handle this properly!"

On impulse, Ivan grabbed the knob and gave it a twist. It was unlocked. He pushed it open a crack. "Hello!" he called. "It's Ivan Barker! Anyone here?"

"Ivan, please," Allison begged. "Shut the door, wipe your prints off the knob, and call the police."

Ignoring her, Ivan pushed the door open far enough for a peek inside. To his horror, he discovered there *was* a body. It was lying face-down on the floor only a few feet from the door. Instinctively, he rushed in to check for a pulse.

CHAPTER 5

Jamie paid for the pepper and started out of the store. Checking her watch, she realized she'd have to hurry if she were to get home in time for the early afternoon news. Milton had hinted he might be mentioned on the news in connection with his Paris adventure, and she didn't want to miss it. Stepping onto the parking lot pavement, she made a beeline for her car. As she walked, she noticed a man just getting out of an SUV. What caught her eye was the unusual way he was dressed. He had on a full-length overcoat and a wide-brimmed hat, a combination that reminded her of the character portrayed in the old movie *The Shadow*. She had to suppress a laugh. She might be more understanding if he were a teenager looking for attention, but this man was no teenager. Maybe he was an actor who hadn't taken time to change out of his costume.

Catching her off guard, the man slowly turned to look directly at her. As he did, she caught sight of something that made her recoil with revulsion. Even with his hat pulled low, she could tell the entire left side of his face had been burned. She instantly looked away, embarrassed to have been caught staring. Hearing footsteps, she glanced back just enough to notice he had stepped away from his vehicle and was headed straight toward her. She stiffened with anxiety but just kept walking, eyes fixed on her car. A sense of shame washed over her as she realized it was his disfigurement that triggered her concern. Under other conditions, she would have paid no attention to someone entering her path.

Jamie slowed her step in hopes he'd pass her by, but all such thoughts vanished when he came within feet of her and spoke her name. "Excuse me, Jamie. I don't mean to frighten you, but we need to talk."

Freezing in her tracks, Jamie stood staring dumbfounded at the man. How could he know her name? She was certain she had never seen him before. Squaring her shoulders and drawing a quick breath for courage, she responded. "I'm afraid you have me at a disadvantage, sir. You obviously know me, but I can't place you. Have we met?"

"Let me put your mind at ease," he very calmly stated. "I'm no one you need to fear. In fact, I'm someone who can be of great benefit if you'll only listen to what I have to say. You see, Jamie, I know some things about your father I think you may find very interesting."

Jamie's heart was still pounding. The only other part of the man's body visible outside his heavy clothing were his hands. She noticed the skin on his left one was also badly burnt. Again, she was gripped with shame for allowing herself to be frightened of this man because of his scars. Forcing herself to relax, she stepped closer to him. "Are you a friend of my father?" she questioned.

"Let's just say I know some things about Ivan," the man explained, his voice remaining calm and reserved. "For instance, I know you're not his first daughter."

Jamie nearly dropped the package she was holding. "What?!" she gasped.

"Rene was born when Ivan was twenty-four. She was a beautiful child whom he and her mother adored."

"Her name was Rene?" Jamie interrupted, unable to grasp the reality of Ivan having another daughter.

The man nodded and continued. "Rene was their only child. When she was just ten, her mother died."

"I know about Allison," Jamie explained quietly. "But I certainly didn't know about Rene." Jamie couldn't understand how she could have a sister she had never met, unless . . . "Is Rene still living?" she asked.

"No, Rene was brutally murdered several years ago. Twenty-five years, to be exact."

Jamie felt her legs nearly buckle under her weight. "Rene was murdered," she gasped. "No wonder my father doesn't want to talk about his past." All apprehension gone now, Jamie wanted to know more. "Tell me about the murder," she pressed. "How did it happen?"

The man pulled down on the brim of his hat, lowering it on his face. "She was kidnapped along with her five-year-old son. The two of them were held for a half-million-dollar ransom. Your father paid the ransom, but it didn't matter."

"Rene had a son? And he was kidnapped along with her?"

"The boy's name was Lance. Thanks to Rene's bravery and quick thinking, Lance escaped with his life. She wasn't so lucky."

Jamie's head was spinning. Her emotions were raw. She was barely able to absorb what she was hearing. The stranger, who obviously noticed, reached out a sympathetic hand and placed it on her shoulder. "I'm so sorry," he softly whispered. "I know how devastating this must be. Once I've explained my reason for telling you these things, I hope you'll understand and forgive me."

"I'll be all right," she assured him. "Please go on."

The man pulled back his hand and adjusted the collar of his coat a little tighter around his neck. "Before going any further, I think it might be well to point out I'm not exactly a stranger to you either, Jamie. I'm aware of the tragedy with your biological parents that led to Ivan adopting you. I also know you're a partner in a private investigation firm."

This revelation stirred a new emotion in Jamie. Pulling herself up to her full five-foot-three, she stared at him through blazing eyes. "Who are you?" she demanded. "How do you know the things you do about my father's past, and what gives you the right to dig into my life?"

Jamie noticed her raised voice had attracted the attention of some others in the parking lot, but she didn't really care. The stranger, on the other hand, did seem bothered by the unwanted attention. "Perhaps we should find a more private place to continue this conversation," he suggested.

Jamie worked her way around the man and again headed toward her car. "We have nothing further to discuss," she stated curtly.

"Rene's murder was never solved," the man called after her.

Jamie stopped and slowly turned to face him again. "What?" she asked in a more subdued voice.

"That's my reason for approaching you."

He hurriedly caught up to her, and together they walked in the direction of her car. "What exactly is it you want from me?" she cautiously asked. In her own mind she had already reasoned his intentions were to link Rene's unsolved murder to her profession as a P. I. She wasn't sure just how, but it was enough to pique her curiosity. Enough so that her anger toward this man lessened considerably.

"What I'm proposing," he cooly stated, "is a new look at Rene's case through the eyes of today's technology."

Jamie considered this. In a way she was flattered that this man, whoever he was, might think her qualified enough to take a new look at Rene's case. But that sort of thing really wasn't up her alley as a P. I. "I like the idea of taking another look at Rene's case," she proposed. "But I'm not trained in forensic criminal science. I'm willing to dig out the old files and go through them, but I'm not sure how much good I can do."

"What would you think of the idea of teaming up with someone who is trained in forensic criminal science?" the man suggested, catching Jamie by surprise.

"Do you have someone in mind?" she asked.

Jamie watched as the man retrieved a pen and notepad from his jacket pocket. He scribbled something on the pad, then pulled off the top sheet and handed it to her. "This is the address of a brand-new forensic laboratory here in Mesa. The person I have in mind to team up with you on Rene's case is there now. It might come as a shock when I tell you who he is."

Jamie glanced at the address on the sheet of paper. It was only a few blocks away. "I'm listening," she said. "Who is he?"

"His name is Lance," the man explained. "Lance Gentry. And before you ask, yes, Lance Gentry is Rene's son."

Jamie shook her head in disbelief. "How many more revelations do you plan to drop on me?" she quipped. "Are you saying Lance Gentry lives right here in Mesa? If so, why haven't I met him?"

"Lance lives in Orlando, Florida. He's a forensic investigator on the police force there. He's here on a leave of absence."

Here was another thing Jamie needed to sort out. "If my father has a grandson living in Florida, why was I never told?" she questioned.

By this time they had reached Jamie's car. She paused by the door but didn't open it yet. "What you're asking gets a little complicated, Jamie," the man explained. "In a nutshell, Rene and Ivan had a falling-out before Lance was even born. There were bad feelings between them, bad enough that Rene made it clear her son was never to have anything to do with his grandfather. Sadly, this became her death wish."

None of this made any sense to Jamie. Ivan was a perfect father. How could there have been problems between him and Rene? There had to be more to this story. Maybe the time had come for her to do some serious digging into Ivan's past in the interest of his own defense, if for no other reason. "So who raised Lance?" she asked. "His father?"

"Actually, no. Lance never knew his father. He was raised by Allison's brother, Charley Stapleton."

Allison had a brother? Here was another tidbit she had never been told.

"Charley raised Lance because Rene wanted it that way," the stranger went on saying. "She didn't want Ivan involved, and the boy's father was killed in Vietnam."

Things were coming at Jamie so fast she hardly had time to duck one bombshell before the next one fell. "What was his father's name?" she asked.

The man held up a hand, cutting her off. "I've already said more about this part than I intended to," he declared. "You're a top-notch investigator, Jamie. I'm sure you can dig out all the details on your own, given time."

Jamie had several questions but something in the man's demeanor told her he had given out all the family history he was going to. She focused her attention in a different direction. "If Lance is as good a forensic investigator as you say he is, why would he need my help?"

"That's a fair question. Lance is good at what he does, but he doesn't know his way around Mesa. Not only that, he doesn't have the necessary contacts here to get the job done. You, on the other hand, know the place inside and out, and you have contacts everywhere. Obviously, the two of you will make the perfect team."

"All right. Assuming I agree to what you're asking, are you going to introduce me to Lance?"

The man smiled. "I've given you the address to his lab and told you he's there now. The rest is up to you. Oh, and by the way, he is expecting you."

"He's expecting me?" Jamie asked in surprise. "You were pretty sure of yourself, weren't you? What if I'd turned you down?"

"You forget, Jamie, I did my homework. I know the kind of person you are. I knew you wouldn't turn me down. One thing, though. I didn't tell Lance your name. You know, just in case you fooled me. Lance knows only that a young woman will be contacting him to help with the case."

Jamie looked this man right in the eye. "You've evidently gone to a lot of trouble setting up this investigation. May I at least ask why? And while we're at it, how about telling me your name."

Again the man smiled. "I haven't told you my name, have I?"

"No, and you haven't told me what your interest in all this is, either."

The man's chest rose and fell with a heavy breath. "Will it make any difference in your decision to help with the case if I choose to remain anonymous?"

Jamie continued looking at him. "I suppose not," she admitted. "Are you saying you do choose to remain anonymous?"

"I'm sorry, but I do have my reasons. Now if you'll excuse me, I probably should be going so you can get to the lab and meet your new partner."

"Just like that? You fill my basket with all this new information, then just turn and walk away?"

He shrugged. "Look at it this way—it adds a hint of intrigue."

"Frankly, I'd rather have answers than intrigue."

"You have a lot more answers than you had fifteen minutes ago, Jamie. Now I really should be going."

Jamie watched as the man tipped his hat, then turned and walked back to his SUV. As he walked, she noticed something she hadn't before. He had the kind of limp she had seen in others with a prosthetic leg. She guessed that at some time in his life, this man had lived through a horrible accident, one that left him severely scarred and apparently severed a leg. She continued watching as he started his vehicle, gave her a final wave, then drove away.

Climbing into her Honda, she tossed the grocery sack on the seat and mapped out in her mind the easiest way to get to the lab where Lance Gentry would be working.

CHAPTER 6

As Ivan knelt near the body, contemplating his next move, a sudden motion caught his eye. He glanced up to see a man wearing a ski mask leap out from behind the sofa and dart toward him at a dead run. Not knowing what to expect, Ivan bounded to his feet. The man caught Ivan completely off guard when he threw something at him. Instinctively, Ivan grabbed the object and watched as the man bolted for a door leading to the garage.

"Stop!" Ivan shouted as the man flung open the door and rushed through it.

Ivan looked at Allison, who harshly chided him. "Why didn't you listen to me? Now look at the mess you've gotten yourself into! You're not only standing over the body of a murder victim, you're holding the murder weapon."

For the first time, Ivan realized the object the man had thrown at him was a revolver. The sound of the garage door opening reached his ears, and he knew the killer was about to make his escape. Ivan bounded for the door and rushed into the garage just in time to see the man in the mask mounting a large, green Kawasaki. Ivan's eyes moved to where the license plate should have been only to discover it was covered over with rags and tape. This man was clearly the real murderer, and he was about to get away. Ivan quickly considered his options. He had to do something, and he had to do it fast. Raising the revolver, he shouted, "Stop right there!"

The engine on the big bike roared to life and the man shoved the foot lever down, placing the bike in first gear. "I said hold it!" Ivan shouted again. "I will use this gun if I have to!"

For one chilling moment, the man looked right at Ivan. His eyes were filled with fiery hatred. "Go ahead, Barker! Shoot me if you can! I'm betting you're too yellow to pull that trigger!" A chill shot through Ivan as he recognized the voice as the one who had called him earlier, directing him to come here to Wagner's house.

The man gave a twist on the grip with his gloved hand. The rear tire spun wildly against the cold pavement, emitting a cloud of blue smoke along with an ear-splitting squeal. Instantly, the bike shot forward. Ivan lowered the pistol until his sights lined up perfectly in the center of the man's back, where he carefully squeezed off a shot. The man never flinched as the bike roared down the driveway and onto the street, where it made an abrupt left turn and vanished out of sight behind a neighboring hedge.

Ivan, who was an expert marksman with a revolver, couldn't believe what had just happened. No way could he have missed with that shot. And even if the man had been wearing a bulletproof vest, there would have been some evidence of the bullet striking its mark.

Then it hit him. This whole thing was a blatant attempt to frame him for Wagner's murder. The killer had anticipated Ivan might get off a shot when he tossed him the gun. He must have placed one blank cartridge in the revolver. Not only would this make Ivan's shot harmless, it would also leave traces of powder on Ivan's hand, giving evidence he had, in fact, fired the gun. Just one more piece of the puzzle being formed to make Ivan appear to be the real killer.

The sound of an approaching siren brought Ivan out of his daze. Seconds later, a police car pulled up in front of the place. "Why wouldn't you listen to me?" Allison moaned, her voice cracking with emotion. "I tried to warn you, but you just wouldn't listen!"

The cold, hard reality of what Allison was saying reached Ivan with horrifying impact. He was wise enough to realize just how serious the mound of evidence stacked against him really was. No way would he want to face a jury who had heard this much evidence against one of his clients. Helplessly, he watched as two officers stepped from the patrol car with guns drawn. "Ivan Barker?" one of them questioned loudly. "What's going on here? We're responding to a 911 call."

Ivan very carefully placed the gun on the ground at his feet. "There's a body inside the house," he said. "And I think you'll find he was killed with this gun."

CHAPTER 7

Jamie checked the number on the door of the lab against the number on the note given to her by the stranger. This was the place. She gave four quick raps on the door. Seconds later, it opened, revealing a man in a white lab apron holding a beaker half filled with some sort of pink liquid. "May I help you?" he asked.

Jamie assumed this man must be Lance Gentry, but she couldn't be sure. She feigned a smile, trying to hide the discomfort she felt at this awkward introduction. "I'm Jamie Barker. I was looking for . . ." She hesitated, searching for the right words, which seemed to leave her at the moment. "That is—I was told I could find Lance Gentry here." Those certainly weren't the right ones. She mentally kicked herself.

"You're in the right place," he confirmed. "I'm Lance."

Jamie studied him for a short time. He was taller than she, about the same height as Milton, she calculated. But that's as far as the comparison went. Milton's hair was light, and he had blue eyes. Lance, on the other hand, had jet black hair and eyes to match. Milton also wore glasses, whereas Lance did not. There was something else about him she couldn't quite put her finger on. If her first introduction was hard, this next part was even worse. "I was told you'd be expecting me." She felt dumb, but how else could she say it?

Lance's eyes lit up. "Oh, then you're? . . . That is? . . ." Lance backed away a step. "Yes, I was expecting you. Please, won't you come inside?"

Jamie stepped in, and Lance closed the door. "Would you like to sit down?" he asked, pulling out a lab stool. "Unfortunately, this is the best I have to offer."

"No, this is fine, I'll just stand. I'm not sure how much you know about me, or if you even know why I'm here."

"What do I know about you?" Lance responded. "Well, let's see . . . according to my source, you're here to help me reopen a quarter-century-old murder case. To tell the truth, that's about all I do know."

"I see," Jamie replied, a little surprised he didn't know more. Glancing around, Jamie was more than a little surprised at the amount of equipment in the lab, all state of the art. She swallowed and looked back at Lance. This was an awkward situation that wasn't showing signs of improving. "I suppose that brings us to the point of what I know about you?" she said, for lack anything better to use as an icebreaker.

"I suppose."

"Well, for starters, I know the murder case you're referring to is your own mother's. That is, if my source was correct."

Lance nodded. "So far, so good . . ."

"I know your mother's name was Rene Gentry, and I know her maiden name was Barker." Jamie thought she noticed Lance tense at mention of the name *Barker*.

"Yes, she was a Barker," he replied uneasily. "You said your name is Barker?" Both brows arched as he posed the next question. "Coincidence or otherwise?"

Jamie brushed a strand of hair away from her eyes. "Not exactly a coincidence," she stated. "You see, Lance, your grandfather and my father are the same man."

The beaker slipped from Lance's hand. It struck the floor, shattering into a pool of splintered glass and pink liquid. "Oh!" he groped, his eyes shifting back and forth between the spill and Jamie. "I—I'm sorry. It's just that . . ." He glanced down at her feet. "I hope it didn't splash on you."

Jamie looked down to check her feet and pant legs. "Looks like I'm pretty dry," she said with a slight laugh, trying to ease his embarrassment. "I hope that pink stuff wasn't something important."

Lance grabbed a handful of rags off the bench just behind him. "No, it was nothing," he said nervously as he knelt to swab up the spill. "I was just testing out some equipment." He tossed the first rag into a nearby trash can, then went on swabbing with a second. "This is very embarrassing. It's just that I didn't know my grandfather had married again."

"Oh, no!" Jamie quickly corrected. "Dad never married again. He adopted me after Allison died."

Lance stood and threw the second rag in the trash can. He used another to wipe his hands. "I didn't know. But then, I know very little of anything about my grandfather. I've never even met him."

"I know—that seems strange to me," Jamie alluded. "But there are many things about my dad I don't understand. He never talks about his life before I came along. I only found out about you less than an hour ago. And then, it was from a complete stranger."

Lance discarded the final towel and faced Jamie again, a look of curiosity filling his eyes. "Let me get this straight; you heard about me from some stranger you met barely an hour ago?"

"Sounds like the plot out of a spy movie, doesn't it?" she jested, trying to further ease the tension that was gradually letting up. "But that's the way it happened."

Lance shifted his weight. "Could you describe this stranger for me?" he asked.

Jamie thought she heard something more than casual curiosity in Lance's voice. "Is there a reason you'd like me to describe him?" she pressed.

"Am I that transparent?" Lance asked, wearing a foolish grin.

"Yes," she responded.

"Well, you're right, I have a very good reason for being interested in your stranger. You see, Jamie, I think he may be the same person who told me about you. Only in my case, all I got was an anonymous letter."

"A letter?"

"Yeah. The same letter that told me about this lab. My anonymous friend is the one footing the bill for it."

The strangeness surrounding this whole series of events grew even more intense as the reality of it formed more clearly in Jamie's mind. If Lance's assumption was right about these two men being one and the same, it would bring up an interesting point. The man was even more secretive with Lance than he had been with Jamie. Lance's only contact came from an anonymous letter. And yet, in spite of the man's elusiveness, he was obviously quite interested in Rene's murder. This was evidenced by his action, if he had indeed financed the forensic lab for the sole purpose of working on her case.

Jamie listened with quickened interest as Lance continued. "This isn't the first dealing I've had with my anonymous friend. He also paid for my education. This man who approached you may be my anonymous benefactor. That's why I'd like to hear you describe him."

Jamie felt torn. She wanted to help Lance, but if the man had gone to this much trouble to remain unknown, did she really have the right to share what little she knew about him? But still, if the man wanted her to keep anything from Lance, he hadn't bothered to make a point of it. The pleading in Lance's eyes was enough to tip the scales. "I met him in a Fry's parking lot," she explained. "I pressed him for a name, but he declined. As for a description—I'd judge him to be somewhere in his midfifties. He's probably five-eight to five-nine and weighs somewhere around 190 pounds. His weight is really hard to judge, since he wore an overcoat. It looked like he'd been in a horrible accident at sometime in his life. From what I could see, the left side of his body was badly burned, and I'm almost certain his left leg is artificial. He also wore a wide-brimmed hat. He could have had other scars underneath his layers." Jamie thought a moment, then said, "That's the best I can do. Does it help?"

Lance rubbed the back of his neck. "Sure it helps, but not as much as I had hoped. The description doesn't ring any bells. I've obviously never met the man, which only adds to the mystery."

"Wait!" Jamie said, remembering the note with the address to the lab on it. "I have something that might be of interest to you." She dug the note out of her purse and handed it to him. "The man wrote your address for me. His fingerprints should be on this note."

Lance's eyes shot open as he took the note from her. "You have fingerprints?" he gasped. "Now there's something I hadn't hoped for."

Jamie watched as Lance moved to a bench containing a computer and several other pieces of equipment. He went right to work without saying another word. He dusted the note with a powder that revealed several prints, some of which Jamie was sure were her own. Lance then photographed the note using a digital camera. Removing the compact flash card from the camera, he plugged it into his computer and brought up a display on the screen. "Yeeesssss!" he shouted. "I think we're on to something here!"

Jamie wondered if Lance would want a sample of her prints in order to distinguish which of the prints on the note were hers and which weren't. Instead, he did something that completely surprised her. He pulled up the sample of a fingerprint already stored in his computer and began overlaying prints until he found an exact match. "Here's the proof!" he shouted. "The man you met in the parking lot and my anonymous benefactor are definitely one and the same." Jamie moved in for a closer look. "The fingerprints on your note match the fingerprints on my letter," Lance explained.

Lance reached into a drawer and removed a letter, which Jamie assumed was the one he had been talking about. He compared it against her note. "The handwriting even matches," he observed. "Do you know what this means? It means he's right here in Mesa. Or at least he was within the past hour." Lance looked up anxiously. "I don't suppose there's a chance he might have suggested a way to contact him?"

Jamie shook off the idea. "I'm sorry."

"Just grasping for straws," he said, exhaling loudly. "Oh well, I'm a lot closer to identifying him than I was before. Do you mind if I keep this note?"

"Help yourself."

Lance tucked the letter and the note away in the drawer and pushed it closed, then asked, "Did he by chance mention I'm a forensic investigator for the Orlando, Florida Police Department?"

"He did. And did he mention to you that I'm a private investigator here in Mesa?"

"No, but that explains his motive for wanting you involved. Can I take it, by your being here, that you are planning to get involved?"

"You don't have a big enough stick to chase me off," she laughingly assured him. "So how about filling in a few gaps? All I know is what I learned from the man in the parking lot, and that's not much."

Lance shoved the mouse aside and spun on his lab stool to face her. "I take it my grandfather—your father—isn't aware you know anything yet?"

"No, he isn't. And I'm not sure what to expect when he does find out. He's gone to a lot of trouble to keep all this from me."

Lance slid off the stool onto his feet. "Maybe we shouldn't tell him just yet."

Jamie wondered if Lance meant this for her sake or for his own. If they were going to reopen Rene's case, Ivan was bound to find out. When he did, there was no way she could keep from admitting what she'd learned. As for Lance, it might be possible for him to slip through without revealing who he was, but it wouldn't be easy with an observant man like Ivan. And for that matter, Jamie wasn't sure she could stand by and allow Lance to do that to her father. After all, her father had the right to know about his own grandson.

"I was five years old," Lance said, moving on into his explanation of the crime. "My mother and I were kidnapped and driven to a log cabin somewhere in the White Mountains. We were held in a room with a bolted door and bars on the only window while the kidnapper went after the ransom. Before he returned, my mother figured out a way to get me out. She wasn't so lucky. Her body was found two weeks later in a dry gulch just off Highway 260. I tried to tell Uncle Charley and the police about the cabin, but there wasn't one anywhere near where they found the body, so they just dropped that part of the investigation." Lance appeared lost in thought for a couple of seconds, then brought up another item. "My Uncle Charley tells me there's a box of evidence from the kidnapping stored away someplace. He heard about it from a friend who used to be a detective with the Mesa Sheriff's Department. His name was Ed Quinn."

"Ed Quinn?" Jamie echoed. "Ed Quinn is the sheriff now. If Ed knows where there's a box of evidence, I won't have any trouble getting my hands on it."

"Fantastic!" Lance exclaimed. "It looks like our friend from the parking lot knew what he was doing when he enlisted your help. And while we're talking about you, may I touch on an observation? I'm not exactly sure how old my grandfather is, but I'd estimate him to be in his late seventies by now. What I'm trying to say is . . ."

"You think I'm a little young to be his daughter?" Jamie guessed, finishing Lance's sentence when he hesitated.

"Something like that, yeah."

"Dad was fifty-eight when he adopted me. Like you, I lost my mother to violence. My father killed her, then turned the gun on himself. I became a ward of the court. That's when your grandfather came to my aid. He waged a terrible battle with the courts to get me.

Being a single father was against him, as well as his age. But he wouldn't give up, and I'm darn glad of it. No one could have had a better father, regardless of any problems the judge was worried about." Jamie glanced up until their eyes met. "I know about your father being killed in the war," she said. "I'm so sorry."

"Yeah, I've always wondered what I missed, never knowing him. I've never even visited his grave, but Uncle Charley's promised to take me there before I head back to Orlando. He's buried here in Phoenix." Lance released a sigh. "So, it seems we both had our share of hard knocks growing up."

"Seems like," Jamie agreed. "Dad came to my rescue, and your Uncle Charley came to yours. Which brings up a question I'd really like help with, if you don't mind. What was the problem between your mother and her dad that resulted in you never knowing him?"

Lance rubbed his mouth skittishly. "I can relate the story if you really want to hear it," he said, speaking very cautiously. "But I have to warn you, it gets pretty graphic."

"I want to hear it," Jamie said, trying to convince herself as well as Lance. She knew it had to be something bad, and learning anything bad about her father wasn't an enticing idea. But the time had definitely come. Putting it off any longer was out of the question after coming this far.

"I have some lemonade made up," Lance said. "I can offer you some if you don't mind drinking out of a beaker."

This brought a smile. "Sounds good."

Lance grabbed a couple of clean beakers and stepped over to the freezer for some ice cubes. This done, he filled the beakers with lemonade taken from the refrigerator. He walked back to the bench, where he handed one beaker to Jamie. Setting his own beaker down, he pulled up two lab stools. "We might as well be as comfortable as possible while we talk," he suggested. Jamie nodded and sat down on one stool. Lance took the other. He began with a question. "How much do you know about my grandmother?"

"Well, let's see. I know her name was Allison, and that she was my dad's childhood sweetheart. They were married eleven years when she died. I think it was cancer."

"Breast cancer," Lance explained. "She was just thirty-two. My mother was ten. According to what Uncle Charley tells me, her death hit Granddad hard, which is probably why he turned into an overly protective parent."

"That's odd," Jamie remarked. "Dad was anything but overly protective with me."

"Maybe he was trying to make up for a few mistakes he made with my mother, you think?"

"That's possible, I suppose. But it's hard for me to conceive Dad ever being overprotective. From the day I entered his life, he allowed me the right to make my own decisions."

Lance shuffled the beaker of lemonade between hands. "According to Uncle Charley, my granddad took it in his head for my mother to become an oncologist. He felt she could give something back to the world in honor of my grandmother that way."

Even though this didn't sound like the Ivan Barker Jamie knew, she could see where it was headed. "Your mother didn't want to be a doctor?" she surmised.

"No, but Granddad refused to let up. He had a client who was the father of an upcoming young heart surgeon named Robert Cranston. Granddad reasoned if he could get Robert and my mother together, things just might work out to build her interest in the medical field. Mom actually dated Robert a few times, but the chemistry just wasn't there. Then, my father came into the picture. He and Mom met at a church social. Dad was in the Air Force, attending pilot school at the time. He was training to be a helicopter pilot. Mom and Dad hit it off instantly, and that was the end of Robert Cranston."

"And Dad couldn't accept this?" Jamie asked, finding it increasingly difficult to envision this side of Ivan.

"That's putting it mildly, Jamie. I'm told he lectured Mom repeatedly on the ills of marrying a military man. It would mean a life with no roots, as Neil would have no idea where he might be assigned from one month to the next. What chance would Mom ever have of earning a medical degree under those circumstances?"

Jamie's thoughts turned to her and Milton. Even if her hunch was right about her father arranging their first meeting, that's as far as his influence had gotten. He never pushed her toward Milton, or any other man, and when she asked his advice about setting a wedding date he simply told her she should follow her heart.

"What I've told you so far is bad enough," Lance continued. "I know you love Ivan, and I know he's been a good father to you, but . . ."

"But if I want to hear the rest of the story, I can expect to hear about a side of Dad I might not like?" she guessed when Lance hesitated.

"I'm really sorry, Jamie. If you'd rather I stop . . ."

"No, please, go on. I have to know."

Lance took a drink of lemonade and replaced the beaker on the table. "I'm sure Granddad thought he was doing the right thing when he took matters into his own hands. As it worked out, my father's commanding officer was another of Granddad's clients. Granddad went to him in confidence and explained he was looking for a way to keep Dad away from Mom. Together, they cooked up a scheme to pull Dad out of pilot training and send him straight into action in Vietnam, where the war was just winding down."

Jamie felt a rush of blood fill her face. "Are you telling me Dad went through with such a thing?"

"I wish I could tell you otherwise, but that's just what happened. To Granddad's chagrin, his plan backfired. Mom and Dad didn't know where the decision to send him into immediate action came from, but when they learned of it, they decided to get married on the spot. Charley tells me when Granddad realized what he had done, he tried to stop the orders, but it was too late. The die was cast, and there was no turning back. They were married three weeks before Dad shipped out. He was killed two months later. He died not knowing Mom was pregnant."

It was not like Lance hadn't warned Jamie before telling her this story, but it didn't make the pain of hearing it any less bitter. How could her dad have done such a thing? More and more she understood why he never talked about his past life.

"Mom discovered the truth about Granddad's interference from one of Dad's military buddies who attended the funeral," Lance further explained. "She was pregnant with me, and from what I'm told, the shock nearly caused her to miscarry. She couldn't bring herself to forgive Granddad. The two of them never spoke again. Uncle Charley took her in and cared for her until I was born. After that, she went to work as a waitress at a Denny's restaurant in Phoenix. Charley leased an apartment and maintained it just for us.

Then, with Mom gone, Charley took me in and raised me like I was his own son."

Lance took another sip of lemonade, then said something Jamie really didn't expect to hear. "I want you to know I don't hate my granddad. I'm not saying I condone what he did, but I can understand what motivated him."

Jamie's eyes filled, blurring her vision. "Thank you for telling me that. It means a lot."

"I'm sorry to say Uncle Charley doesn't share my feelings, Jamie. I've never heard him say many good things about Granddad."

At that moment they were interrupted by the sound of Jamie's cell phone ringing. "Excuse me," she sniffed, brushing her eyes before digging the phone out of her purse. "It's Dad," she said, glancing at the caller ID. "I wonder what's up." She pressed the receive button. "Hi, Dad."

"Listen, Jamie, I don't want you upset, but I'm down at police headquarters. I have a bit of a problem, it seems."

Hearing her father was at police headquarters came as no surprise to Jamie. He often went there on behalf of some client. It was the part about him having a problem that concerned her. "I'm listening, Dad. What's the problem?"

"Well, you see, there's been a mistake. I've been arrested."

"Arrested!" she cried in alarm. "On what charge?"

"Let's not worry about the charge right now," he said, obviously trying to calm her. "As I said, it's all a mistake. They're in the process of booking me now, and this is the one phone call I'm allowed by law."

"I can be there in fifteen minutes, Dad. Have they set bail yet?"

Jamie heard her father release a long sigh. "There's no use in your coming to the station. They probably won't let you in to see me anyway. And as for bail, that's not an option. I'm being held without bail."

"You're what?" she shrieked. "Daddy, you tell me this instant! What are the charges?"

"I'll explain everything later, Jamie. Right now, here's what I need you to do. Contact Sidney Manson and have him get down here right away. This whole thing is a mix-up, and I need Sidney's help to get everything sorted out."

Sidney Manson was a colleague working at the same law firm as Ivan. Jamie knew she'd have no trouble reaching Sidney, but she wasn't of a mind to end this call without knowing a lot more than she knew right now. She glanced at Lance to see a look of concern on his face. "Listen to me, Dad!" she persisted. "I demand to know what this is all about! Are you going to tell me, or am I going to have to find out on my own? You know I'm a good enough investigator to find out anything when I set my mind to it!"

"All right, all right!" Ivan reluctantly conceded. "You know I've been working on the Samuel Wagner case. He was the one accused of killing Billy Ray Swineheart."

"Was?" Jamie countered, not missing the verb tense in her father's remark.

"Yeah—was. Samuel ended up a victim himself. I stopped by his place to discover he had been murdered. I even caught a glimpse of the killer, but he got away just before the police arrived."

Jamie felt the blood drain from her face. "The police are trying to pin his murder on you—that's what this is about, isn't it?"

"That about sums it up, Jamie. But they can't make it stick. I didn't do it, and we'll prove it. That's why I need Sidney here ASAP."

Jamie wiped at her eyes. "I swear, you'll do anything to get out of eating my roast beef, won't you?"

"You know better than that, Jamie. I demand a rain check as soon as possible. Oops, I think they want me to hang up now. Make that call to Sidney, okay?"

"Yes, yes, I'll call him, Daddy."

Jamie heard the line go dead, then looked back at Lance. "I gather that wasn't a good-news call," he observed.

"My dad's been arrested for murder. I have to call his attorney." Jamie quickly punched in the number for her dad's office, where she had the best chance of catching Sidney.

"Countryside Office Firm," came a voice Jamie recognized as Mildred Cook, her father's legal secretary.

"Mildred! Jamie here! I need to speak with Sidney, is he handy?"

"He just happens to be standing here right beside me," Mildred answered. "I'll hand him the phone."

"Hi, Jamie," Sidney replied just seconds later. "What's up?"

"I need you to get down to the police station fast!" she said hurriedly. "Dad's been arrested for Samuel Wagner's murder!"

"He's been what? Are you serious, Jamie?"

"Yes, I'm serious. He used his one call with me."

"All right! I'll have Mildred cancel everything, and get down there as soon as I can. I have just one stop I have to make on the way but I'll keep it short, I promise, Jamie. And don't worry. Mistakes like this happen all the time. We'll get it straightened out."

"Thanks, Sidney. Keep me posted, okay?"

"Will do. Just keep your cell phone on."

Jamie considered calling Milton but decided against it. Milton had enough on his mind at the moment trying to dig out from his Paris trip and at the same time fight his jet lag. She dropped the phone back in her purse

"My grandfather's been accused of murder?" Lance asked. "Fill me in on the details, Jamie."

"All I know is he's been accused of killing one of his own clients, a Samuel Wagner. Curiously enough, Samuel himself was facing a murder rap that Dad felt was a frame-up."

"Did this murder happen recently?" Lance asked.

"It seems that way. Dad was arrested at the scene."

"Okay, next question. Do you have enough clout with the local police to get me onto that crime scene?"

Jamie suddenly realized where Lance was headed with this. "You're offering to help Dad, aren't you?"

"I am if you can get me into the crime scene. I'm an outsider here, you know."

"You're darn right I can get you on the scene," Jamie assured. "I already told you Sheriff Quinn is a good friend of mine. All it will take is one call."

"Forget the phone call, let's go talk to Quinn in person. We can kill two birds with one stone if he'll let us talk to Granddad."

"Two birds? You're referring to the box of evidence for your mother's case as the second bird, I presume."

"Right on! You do have a car, don't you?"

"Yes, I have a car."

"Good. Let me gather up a few things, then we can be on our way. I think it's time I met my long-lost grandfather."

CHAPTER 8

Ivan was no stranger to a jail cell—not when it came to visiting a client, that is. But this business of being confined in one himself was a new and unpleasant experience. Flopping down on the iron bunk, he rubbed his eyes as if that might magically make this whole thing go away. When he opened his eyes again, he saw Allison's smiling face staring back at him. "Thank heavens you're here," he told her. "If ever I needed your cheering up, it's now."

"You want me to cheer you up? That's a lovely request. If you'd listened to me in the first place, you wouldn't be in this mess."

Ivan sat up on the edge of the bunk. "There's something I don't understand, Allison," he said, paying no attention to her chastising. "How is it possible you knew about Samuel's body even before I opened his door? I just don't get it!"

"What is it you don't understand? I'm an angel. Closed doors mean nothing to me."

Ivan twisted his head to one side, trying to work some of the stiffness out of his neck. He was about to tell Allison she wasn't a real angel when they were interrupted by someone slipping a key in his cell lock. Ivan glanced around to see his old friend Sheriff Quinn enter the cell. "I just got word!" Quinn exclaimed. "I was down at city hall when they brought you in. What's the story here?"

"I'm being set up, Ed," Ivan responded without the slightest hesitation. "Whoever this guy is, he's doing a good job of it." Ivan glanced at Allison. "I have to admit, I've played right into his hands." She smiled and winked. He got the message.

"But you *are* innocent, right?" Quinn reacted.

Ivan wet his lips. "Do you really have to ask, Ed?"

Quinn brushed a spot of dirt off Ivan's shoulder. "Not personally. But professionally, you know it's my job."

"Well, Ed, you can put your mind at ease. I didn't kill Samuel Wagner, and I will find a way to prove it."

"I believe you, Ivan. Which brings us to point two of why I'm here. You have a couple of visitors. Give me your word you'll behave and I'll forego the cuffs."

A couple of visitors? Ivan was expecting Sidney Manson, but he had no idea who might be with him. No big deal, he'd learn who it was momentarily. "You have my word, Ed. If I try busting out of here, I won't do it on your shift"

"My office is a lot more comfortable than this cell. Come on, you can meet with your visitors there."

Ivan managed a laugh. "You're letting an accused murderer meet his lawyer in your office? You better hope the press doesn't get wind of this."

"Who's going to tell them, you?"

"Yeah, right. Thanks, Ed, it's a thoughtful gesture."

As they stepped into the sheriff's office, Ivan was surprised to see it wasn't Sidney at all. It was Jamie and a young man he didn't know. Jamie rushed over and threw her arms around his neck. She didn't speak but just clung to him very tightly with tears streaming down her face.

"I wasn't expecting you," Ivan finally said. "I thought Sidney was coming."

Jamie took a step back and looked Ivan over closely. "You're not hurt are you, Dad?" she asked.

"No, Jamie, I'm not hurt. I'm fine, other than being set up for killing one of my own clients. Is Sidney on his way?"

"He said he had one stop to make, but yes, he's on his way. I want to hear the whole account of this thing just the way it happened. But first, I have someone I'd like you to meet, Daddy." Jamie took Ivan by the arm and led him over to Lance. "This is Lance. I want him to hear your story too."

"Pleased to meet you, sir," Lance said, extending a hand.

Ivan accepted the handshake with strong curiosity. Who was this fellow, and why had Jamie brought him here? Ivan wasn't sure whether he was imagining it or not, but it seemed to him the young man's eyes were burning holes through him. Even before the hand-shake ended, Jamie broke into her explanation. "Lance is a forensic criminal investigator, Dad. He's agreed to help me prove your innocence. Sheriff Quinn here has already given us permission to visit the crime scene, but we want to hear your side of what happened first."

"I can step out of the room if you like," Quinn suggested.

"No!" Ivan quickly countered, all the while trying to sort this out. "Anything we have to say can be said in front of you, Ed. Please stay."

Quinn nodded, closed the door, then moved to the large window overlooking the general office area and pulled the shade closed. "Just in case we have any lip-readers out there," he joked.

Ivan glanced at Jamie. "I figured you'd jump on the bandwagon sooner or later. Looks like you decided on sooner." Turning to Lance, he asked, "Are you new to the area? I thought I knew all the investigators in these parts."

Again, Jamie jumped in. "Lance is a police officer from Florida, Dad. He's here working on a special case of his own. When he heard about your dilemma, he offered to pitch in."

"That's right, sir. I'll be more than glad to do what I can. That is, if you want my help."

Ivan was sure he detected a hint of uneasiness in Lance's voice. He couldn't shake the feeling there was something curious about this man. Suddenly he was gripped by an intriguing thought. Somewhere out there in this big world, Ivan had a grandson named Lance. Oddly enough, Ivan's grandson would even be about the age of this young man. "I appreciate all the help I can get, son," Ivan told him. Then he decided to act on a hunch. "By the way, what did you say your last name was?"

"Smith!" Jamie broke in, sounding strangely nervous.

Lance looked questionably at Jamie, than back to Ivan. "Yes," he confirmed. "I'm Lance Smith. I've brought some equipment along with me. Would you mind if I check to see if you've fired a weapon recently?"

"That won't be necessary, son. I admit firing the murder weapon, just not at the victim."

"You fired the murder weapon?" Jamie blurted out.

"Yeah. I came face-to-face with the killer, and he threw the gun at me. I caught the blasted thing without thinking. I took a shot, but he'd outguessed me, it seems. The best I can figure is, he'd inserted a blank cartridge in the chamber."

Lance closed his bag. "In that case, I'll leave it to the police to make the test. But I do want to hear your story, starting with your reason for being at Wagner's house in the first place."

For the first time since entering the sheriff's office, Ivan noticed Allison. To his amazement, she wasn't looking at him at all—she was looking at young Lance. And her eyes were watery. Ivan considered it in greater depth. Lance Smith? He could only wonder. But for now, he'd put those feelings on hold and tell his story.

CHAPTER 9

Jamie pulled her Honda to a stop across the street from the crime scene. She and Lance exited the car and approached the officer patrolling the boundaries that had been marked off with yellow crime-scene tape. "Hi," she said to the officer. "We're the two investigators Sheriff Quinn called ahead about."

The officer stood his ground. "I recognize you, Miss Barker, but I'll need to see some identification from your friend."

Lance showed the officer his badge from the Orlando Police Department. "That's nice," the officer countered. "But this isn't Florida. How about something with your picture on it? A driver's license will do nicely."

Lance pulled his license from his wallet and handed it to the officer, who looked it over closely. "All right," the officer said, returning the license. "Go ahead. The crew inside has instructions to give you the run of the place."

"Sorry about that," Jamie said as the two of them crossed the lawn on their way to the front door. "He's one of our newer officers."

"Just doing his job," Lance responded. "Can't slight him for that."

They stepped through the door, where they spotted Samuel's body still lying where he had fallen. This was Lance's first stop. He handed Jamie a pair of latex gloves and slid a pair on himself. As he bent down to check the body, Jamie glanced across the room at Don Simon, the officer in charge of the investigation. "Been expecting you," Don called over to her. "Let me know if you need anything."

"Thanks, Don," Jamie called back. Turning her attention to Lance, she watched as he checked the wound over closely, then painstakingly calculated the angle of entry for the fatal bullet. Removing a clean swab from his kit, he took a blood sample, which he placed in a plastic bag to be analyzed back at his lab. Next he focused his attention on the victim's right hand. "Look at this," he said, calling Jamie's attention to the hand. She bent down for a closer look as he explained. "The shape of the fingers make it appear Samuel was holding something when he died. I'm betting it was a gun, which the killer later removed." Jamie was amazed at how Lance had reached this conclusion simply from the way the victim's hand looked.

Lance opened his bag and removed an aerosol can from it. "Maybe we'll get lucky," he said. "If Samuel did have a gun, he might have gotten off a shot." Lance aimed the aerosol can at the victim's hand and gave it a spray. He also shot a spray toward the front of the victim's shirt. "Well, would you look at this. We have residue on the hand and on the shirt. Our boy did fire a gun."

Lance stood and glanced around the room. "I'm guessing there's at least one bullet from his gun someplace in this room."

"A bullet shouldn't be too hard to find," Jamie observed.

"You're probably right. Let me take a few pictures here, and we'll make a search."

Lance removed a camera from his bag of tricks and snapped off several shots of the body from different angles. Hanging the camera around his neck, he again glanced at the rest of the room. "Why don't you start at that wall over there?" he said, pointing. "I'll start on the opposite side of the room."

Noticing they were on to something, Don Simon walked over to join them. "So, what's up? Are you two looking for anything specific?"

"Your boy over here fired a weapon shortly before he cashed it in," Lance explained, motioning toward the body. "There's a bullet here someplace, I'll stake my reputation on it."

"He fired a gun, eh?" the officer responded, obviously with sharpened interest. "Me and the boys will help you look." His voice raised a level. "Listen up, gang! We have reason to believe there's a bullet lodged someplace in this room. Let's add some eyes to the search, okay?"

"I may be able to speed things up some," Jamie suggested. "Dad said the killer was hiding behind that sofa over there when he came in the room. Maybe the guy was there when he confronted Samuel too. It's just a thought, but it might be a good place to start."

"Good thinking," Lance exclaimed, heading straight for the sofa, where he started checking one end while Jamie checked the other.

"Here," Jamie said after only a few seconds. "Have a look, Lance."

Lance moved over to her end, where she pointed out a small tear in the fabric near the edge of the arm. "It does look suspicious," he agreed upon a closer check. "It looks like the hole may go all the way through." Gripping the arm of the sofa, he pulled it a few inches away from the wall. "Bingo!" he cried. "We have a bullet lodged in the wall! Great work, Jamie!"

She glanced over his shoulder to see where the bullet had buried itself in the wall just as Don Simon moved in for a look of his own. "Well, I'll be darned," Don sounded. "You nailed that one, buddy."

Lance answered with a nod and made an observation. "The sofa slowed the bullet enough to keep it from burying too deeply, so it should still be in pretty good shape. Do you mind if I remove it from the wall, Don?"

"This was your discovery, pal. Make the most of it. I'll need to keep the bullet for my lab people, naturally."

"Yeah, right. I want to start by checking the sofa before I remove the bullet."

Jamie watched with interest as Lance meticulously checked the fabric one inch at a time. Without question, he knew what he was doing—and he obviously loved his work. He had a way of tuning out the rest of the world while focusing on one tiny detail of evidence. Only when he was satisfied he had gleaned all he could from one detail did he move on to the next. After spending a full five minutes examining the bullet hole in the sofa, he spoke up. "It looks like our boy Samuel hit what he was aiming at, Jamie. There's traces of blood on the sofa, and I'm betting we find blood on the bullet."

"The killer was shot?" Jamie questioned in surprise. "Dad didn't mention that."

"Could be the whole thing happened so fast Granddad just failed to notice," Lance calculated. "But my guess is it was only a superficial flesh wound that wouldn't have been all that apparent." Lance moved around the sofa and assumed a position he felt the killer might have taken at the time he fired the fatal shot. "If the killer was here," Lance went on, "and if he was holding his gun with his left hand, that would put the path of his bullet that killed Samuel exactly right. And it would put the killer's right arm at this point." Again, Lance demonstrated. "As you can see, a bullet fired by Samuel would pass through the flesh of the killer's upper arm and enter the sofa at the precise angle we've discovered. This leads me to two assumptions. First, the killer's probably left-handed, and second—he probably has a flesh wound on his right arm."

Jamie was amazed at how much Lance had gotten from such a seemingly small clue. If he in fact did have a blood sample of the killer, it could prove even more valuable than a set of fingerprints, thanks to what could be done with DNA testing these days. Lance moved to the wall where the bullet was lodged. "I was right," he noted even before extracting the bullet. "We do have blood traces." Lance took more swab samples, then carefully dug the bullet out. "A .45 caliber," he remarked, dropping it in a plastic bag, which he handed to Don Simon. "I'd like a copy of your lab's findings on this if that's okay," he said. "And a copy of the autopsy report if I might."

"I'll see to it," Don promised. "And naturally, we'd like anything you dig up as well."

"Good as done," Lance agreed.

Don rubbed his chin as he studied this displaced police officer with an expertise in forensic science. "What's an investigator from Florida doing with a lab in our parts, if you don't mind my asking?" he quizzed.

"That's a fair question. Ever hear of a kidnap-murder case that went unsolved in these parts some twenty-five years ago?"

Don thought only a moment before venturing a guess. "Rene Gentry, by chance?"

"Yes, Rene Gentry."

"Who around here in police work hasn't heard of Rene Gentry's case? It was a real black mark on our department, letting that one go unsolved."

"Rene Gentry was my mother," Lance explained.

"I see," Don said, his eyes gleaming with interest. "And you intend to reopen your mother's case?"

"Yes."

Don patted Lance on the back. "Anything I can do to help, just ask. And by the way, I have to admit, your work here has changed my mind. From what I saw at first, I had it figured Ivan Barker was guilty as they come. The way I see it now, Ivan's story about being set up makes more sense. If you ever want to leave Florida, I'll be glad to put in a good word at our department."

"Thanks, Don, I'll keep that in mind."

"So, are we finished here?" Jamie asked as Don walked away.

"Not just yet," Lance said. "I'd like to get a look in the garage. Granddad said the killer got away on a motorcycle. Maybe he made a mistake, and with any luck we can pick up on it."

"Mistake?" Jamie asked. "What sort of mistake?"

"Don't know yet, that's why we need to look. It's been my experience that most criminals do make mistakes. They may think of themselves as pillars of intelligence, but the facts speak otherwise. All we have to do is be thorough enough to uncover a mistake, and more often than not, we nail the guy. Come on, let's have a look at the garage."

* * *

Charley Stapleton sat alone in the restaurant booth picking over what was left of the prime rib on his plate. It wasn't unusual for Charley to eat alone at one restaurant or another. It was a habit he'd had longer than he cared to remember. It was a lonesome life but one he had gotten used to over the years. Charley had never married. He almost wanted to once, but things just didn't work out. What kind of life could Charley offer a wife anyway? Bounce here looking for work, bounce there looking for work—certainly not the sort of life any self-respecting woman would choose for herself.

Sometimes Charley still thought about Pat. He often wondered what might have happened if he'd had the courage to ask her to marry him. He almost asked her the night the two of them gave their last performance together in the stage play *Cats*. But when he saw her laughing and joking with the director, Ted Wolf, and even giving the man a playful kiss, he simply walked away and never looked back. He heard through the grapevine she gave up acting and became a helicopter pilot or something. *Imagine that, an actress turned helicopter pilot,* Charley thought. *Will wonders never cease?* Be that as it may, with her out of the acting business, their paths had never crossed again. He hadn't seen her in nearly twenty years.

Charley pushed thoughts of Pat out of his mind and thought instead of Lance and how happy he was to have him this close, even if it wouldn't be for all that long a time. Charley couldn't help but harbor doubts that Lance could ever learn much about his mother's murder—not with the trail being twenty-five-years cold. Twenty-five years? Had it really been that long? Charley took a drink of soda and allowed his mind to drift back to that night he and Detective Ed Quinn had spent on the mountain, crouched side by side behind a fallen tree. That had to be the longest night of his life.

Charley shoved his plate aside, too sick at heart from this memory to eat another bite. He wiped a napkin across his mouth, then smoothed his mustache as thoughts of Rene filled his mind. How thankful he was that she had been wise enough to figure out a way to save Lance's life, even if she couldn't save her own. He stood and walked to the cash register, where he paid the check.

Stepping from the restaurant, he drew in a deep breath of fresh air. In a way it was good, being back in Mesa. He had a lot of memories of this place, some warm and some not so warm. He and his sister, Allison, had grown up in Mesa. He'd seen her married here, and he was here the day Rene was born. All the memories up to that point had been good ones. It was after Allison died that things changed. Charley spent less time in Mesa after that. At least until after Neil was killed. At that time, he returned and leased an apartment for Rene's sake, since she refused to allow Ivan to help her out. Charley stayed pretty close until after Lance was born, then checked in on them from time to time between jobs to be sure they were okay. It was just such a time, when he was in town checking on them, that the kidnapping occurred.

Charley remained there just long enough for the funeral. Then he took Lance away without so much as a second thought about Ivan. After all, it was Rene's wish that Lance be kept away from his grandfather, and Charley intended to honor that wish. Neither he nor Lance had cast another shadow on the streets of Mesa again until this very morning.

Charley had no idea how long Lance would be here working on his mother's case, but as for himself—he planned on a very short stay. The job situation didn't look promising, so he figured it best to hit the road early. Sticking around this town too long had drawbacks, the worst of which would be running into Ivan Barker. That was the last thing Charley wanted.

Slipping behind the wheel of his rental car, he decided on a trip to the grocery store for a few things before retiring to the motel for the night.

CHAPTER 10

From what Jamie had seen of Lance Gentry, she knew she was in the presence of a real professional. Nothing escaped his trained eye. It gave her a feeling of great comfort knowing he was helping on her father's case. As he moved from the house to the garage, she eagerly followed. "I still don't know what we're looking for exactly," she remarked.

"Motorcycle tracks, for one thing," he explained.

"That's right!" Jamie exclaimed. "The tracks could identify a motorcycle as the one used in the getaway, provided, of course, the motorcycle is ever found."

Lance pressed the automatic door opener, raising the door and allowing more light to enter the garage. The first thing he did was snap a few pictures of the tire tread. Next, he knelt down and scraped up a sampling of rubber from the tracks. "This is a long shot," he said. "But, like you've observed, if we find the bike, we'll have two things to help identify it as the right one: the tire tread, plus the composition of rubber in the tire." Filing this sample in his kit, Lance stood and began investigating other parts of the garage.

"What are we looking for now?" Jamie asked.

"Anything that seems out of place. You never know what might turn up if you check close enough." Lance moved to a workbench on one side of the garage and carefully checked every inch of it. Next he surveyed a few tools and other items hanging on the walls. "I don't see anything out of the ordinary here," he stated at last. "Let's take a walk out to the street and have a look."

As they reached the street, they noticed there was just enough tire mark left to indicate the direction the killer had taken in making his escape on the motorcycle. "Well, what have we here?" Lance said abruptly, spotting something white lying next to the curb. He removed a pencil from his shirt pocket and used the end of it to pick up what Jamie noticed was a handkerchief.

"You think that's a clue?" she asked.

"It is if it belonged to the killer."

She shook her head. The handkerchief could have ended up there in any one of a million ways. "How could you possibly know if it belonged to the killer?" she asked.

Lance moved it around where Jamie could get a better look at it. "Take a look," he said. "I think you can answer your own question."

"It has blood on it!" she observed. "If the killer was shot, he might have used the handkerchief to bind his wound."

"Yep. And the wind might have blown it off as he sped away."

"Wait!" Jamie suddenly cried. "Let me guess if this is what you're thinking. If the blood on the handkerchief matches the blood on the bullet, it means the handkerchief pretty much has to belong to the killer."

"That's the way I see it," Lance affirmed. "And look at what else we have, Jamie. This handkerchief is monogrammed with the letters *SJ*. You see what I mean about bad guys making mistakes?"

"You called that one," Jamie laughed. "So, how long will it take to compare the blood samples?"

"Not long once I'm back in the lab."

Now it was Jamie's turn to put her investigative skills to use. "You know what I'm thinking?" she said. "I'm thinking whoever did this went to great lengths to set my dad up. Which points to someone who doesn't like him very much."

Lance's eyes lit up. "Someone he sent to prison somewhere along the way, is that what you're thinking?"

"It only makes sense! Dad's made plenty of enemies over the years in the courtroom. I can't think of a better motive for trying to pin a murder on him."

"Nor can I," Lance agreed. "And if we can find someone on the list of those he's convicted with the initials *SJ*, we have ourselves a pretty sure suspect. Granddad keeps good records, I assume."

"He keeps meticulous records. The problem is, most of his stuff is hard copy. You have to remember, Dad's seventy-five years old. The majority of his career came long before computers."

"Is Granddad really that old?" Lance mused aloud. "After meeting him, I have to say he certainly holds his age well."

"Dad's always taken care of himself. I've tried over and over to talk him into retirement, but he just laughs at me. He says he plans to win his last case on his hundredth birthday. Then he'll retire to fishing the rest of his life. Knowing him, he'll do it, too."

At that moment, Jamie's cell phone rang. She pulled it from her purse and checked to see it was Ivan again. "Yes, Dad, what's up?"

"Sidney showed up, Jamie. He got the judge to set bail and I'm out, but they won't let me have my car. It's evidence. Any chance you can pick me up?"

"Where, at police headquarters?"

"Yeah."

"Sure, Dad. Lance and I are just finishing up our investigation at Wagner's place. You're going to like what we've come up with. We can be there in about twenty minutes."

"I'll be here," he sighed. "Without my car, I'm not going anyplace."

Jamie shut off her phone and dropped it back in her purse. "Dad's out on bail," she explained to Lance. "He needs us to pick him up."

Lance inserted the handkerchief in a plastic bag and shoved it in his pocket. "There's a good chance this has fingerprints on it," he observed. "It's not likely the killer would have used gloves when he put it in his pocket this morning."

"You can get prints off a cloth handkerchief?" Jamie asked.

"It's not easy, but I can do it, trust me. I'd say we're done here, Jamie. Let's go get Granddad."

The two of them crossed the street on their way to Jamie's Honda. As Jamie stepped from the curb, she caught the heel of one shoe and lost her balance, tumbling right into Lance's arms. Her face instantly beamed bright red. Lance gently righted her, then stood smiling. Jamie wished she could just close her eyes and disappear. It was all so embarrassing. But the thing that bothered her even more than the embarrassment was the way she felt for those few seconds she was in Lance's arms. Why had it caused her heart to suddenly race? Why were his eyes burning so deeply into her now? And why did he still have this feeling of familiarity about him? She took a breath and stepped back. "Thank you," she managed. "That was clumsy of me."

"My pleasure," he smiled. Something in his voice made her believe he really meant it. Moments later, they were on their way to police headquarters. It took several minutes for her heart to find its normal pace, and she still could only wonder why.

* * *

"You sure you don't need a ride, Ivan?" Sheriff Quinn asked. "I can have one of the guys run you home."

"Thanks, Ed, but I called Jamie. She's on her way to get me."

"Did she say if they found anything at the crime scene?"

"She hinted they found something I was going to like." Ivan thought a moment, then asked a question of his own. "What do you know about this Lance Smith, Ed? I get the feeling there's more going on with that young man than I'm being told." A worried look crossed Quinn's face, but he didn't respond. "You're in on this, too, aren't you?" Ivan pressed. "Come on, old friend, fill me in! What's going on?"

"Ho, boy," Quinn squirmed. "I had a hunch from the way those two were acting that you didn't know. Then when they introduced him as Smith? . . . Just let me say this, Ivan. Lance is someone you'll probably want to get better acquainted with. But I think he'd be the one to tell you why."

"Ed!" Ivan rebutted. "Have a heart! What's going on here?"

Quinn blew out a long breath. "I'm not going to tell you the whole story, but I will tell you this much. Lance is trying to solve an old case that's still open on our books. He asked me for a box of evidence we've had in storage. I handed it over to him when he was here at the station earlier."

"What old case?" Ivan continued to press. "One I represented?"

Quinn shook his head abruptly. "I've already said too much, Ivan. I'm not saying anymore. You'll have to hear the rest from Lance or Jamie." Quinn waved a finger at Ivan. "And don't you dare let them know you dragged this much out of me. Now, you're welcome to wait in my office for them to pick you up if you like."

Ivan didn't want to back away from the subject, but he was wise enough to know Quinn meant business. "Thanks again," he responded. "But I think I'll wait out front. I need some fresh air, and it'll give me a chance to do some thinking."

Quinn waved his finger again. "Not one word, you hear me!"

"I hear you, Ed," Ivan agreed. "I think it's pretty ornery of you, not filling me in. But I'll honor your wishes."

Ivan stepped from the building to see the sun was just beginning to set. Where had this day gone? As he expected, Allison was waiting for him on the sidewalk right outside the door. "All right," he told her. "I admit I'm glad you've met me here, but I don't want to hear any more *I told you so's*. I concede I should never have set foot in Samuel's house. Now, can we let the subject drop?"

"What's done is done," Allison agreed. "And besides, I have some more exciting news to tell you. I'm really impressed with this young Lance that's helping out with your case."

Ivan's brow wrinkled. "There's something going on with Lance Smith that I don't know about. But I will find out, you can bet on it!"

Allison tossed her head, flinging her hair off one shoulder. "His name isn't Smith," she teased.

"Don't think I haven't got that figured out on my own," Ivan countered. "Smith? I can't believe Jamie would pick that name out of the air and expect me to buy it."

"I know something else about Lance you don't know," Allison added through a feisty grin. "Want to hear it?"

Ivan's heart warmed thinking how much this imagined Allison was like the real Allison. Whenever she had some little tidbit she wanted to pass along, she'd always get that certain sparkle in her voice, just like now. "I'm listening," he said.

"Remember I told you that Milton wasn't the right one for Jamie?"

Ivan eyed her suspiciously. "You also told me the one who was right for her was your little secret, if you'll think back."

"That was true earlier today, but I'm cleared to tell you now. Things have changed just that quickly. Sometimes it works that way in my world of angels."

"Yeah, right. And I bet this is leading up to Lance Smith. That *is* where you're headed, isn't it, Allison?"

Allison beamed. "Yes. The two of them are meant for each other. If all goes according to plan, they'll soon be pledging the very same eternal vows we did all those years ago, Ivan."

Ivan laughed. "You always were a matchmaker in real life, Allison. I suppose it's only fitting your ghost should be one, too. But, need I remind you Jamie is still wearing Milton's ring?"

"A mere temporary setback," Allison grinned. "Lance is the one for Jamie. And Lance is the one who's going to get you off the hook in the Wagner murder case."

"I have to admit, I hope that part of your story is right. If the mysterious Mr. Smith can 'get me off the hook,' as you put it, I'll be forever grateful."

"Grateful enough to welcome him to the family as your son-in-law?"

"Allison! That's Jamie's choice, not mine. I made the mistake of trying to set Rene up with Robert Cranston. I've learned enough to keep my nose out of Jamie's personal life."

Allison's smile grew even larger. "I know the other secret about Lance, too. The one they're all keeping you in the dark about, dear. But I'm forbidden to tell you yet. Just let me say, you'll know before the sun comes up tomorrow morning. What you're about to learn is going to give you a whole new outlook on life."

Ivan scowled at her. "Are you hinting there's something wrong with my outlook now?"

"In a word, yes!" she retorted. "But for now, let me point out that the Honda just rounding the corner is Jamie's."

Ivan looked to see Allison was right. As Jamie pulled up to the curb, the passenger door swung open and Lance stepped out. Pulling the seat forward, he climbed in the back. "You can ride up front with your daughter, sir," he told Ivan.

Ivan slid in the car, closed the door, and snapped his seat belt. He looked at Jamie to see she was offering him a sack of fast food. "I know this isn't the roast beef I promised you tonight, Dad," she said, "but under the circumstances, it'll have to do. I picked up Chinese. I hope that's okay."

"It smells great, baby. I didn't realize how hungry I was. I assume you two have eaten."

Jamie pulled the car back into traffic. "We ate ours on the way. But wait till you hear what we've been up to."

"Listen up, sweetie," a smiling Allison said from the backseat. "You're about to learn just how right I was when I told you you're in good hands." Ivan shot a quick look to see her sitting in the seat next to Lance.

Biting into a bit of sweet and sour chicken, Ivan listened as Jamie started explaining all they had uncovered at Wagner's house. It took several minutes, with Lance filling in some of the details along the way. Ivan was especially interested in the handkerchief with the monogram *SJ* on it. He searched his memory, trying to pull up a name with those initials. "I just can't think of an *SJ*," he told them. "Not in any of my recent cases."

"It doesn't have to be a recent case," Allison cut in for Ivan's benefit, even though the others couldn't hear. "Think back, Ivan. There was an *SJ* several years ago. You helped convict him of murder."

Jamie spoke up. "I know you can't remember every case, but I think you can see how hot this lead is. How big a job would it be to search your files?"

Ivan mulled the idea over in his mind. "Let's put it this way, Jamie. I argued my first case back in 1950. I have detailed files of that case and every case since. My file cabinets fill one entire wall of my office. Offhand, I'd say finding one set of initials might take awhile."

"What sort of system do you use for your filing, Mr. Barker?" Lance asked.

"I have everything filed by the month and year the case was closed."

"Nothing in alphabetical order?" Lance further inquired.

"The only thing I have filed alphabetically is inside each individual case folder. I have a cover sheet in each folder listing the names of everyone involved in that case. That list is alphabetized, but as for the case folders themselves—they're filed by month and year. A search like this could take days. Best scenario possible would put it into hours."

"Unless you have an angel helping with your search," Allison remarked. Ivan glanced at her and just shook his head.

"I'm betting these initials will lead to our man," Lance reiterated "However long it takes, it'll be worth it if it puts a name to our killer. How about it, Mr. Barker? You feel up to losing a night's sleep?"

"I think you know the answer to that, son. Can the two of you pitch in to help?"

"We could, yes. But I think our time would be better spent in my lab. I can get you some help, though. I have a—well, let's just call him a friend who I'm sure wouldn't mind. His name is Charles."

"Take him up on it," Allison said. "You know all your colleagues are tied up with their own cases, and you need to get started on those files right away."

Ivan knew Allison was right. He wished Jamie and Lance would stay with him, but again he realized they could accomplish more in a forensic lab. Having some stranger poking through his files wasn't something Ivan would vote for under normal circumstances, but right now he needed help badly enough to take what he could get. "You're sure this friend won't mind?" he asked Lance.

* * *

Jamie felt a rush of apprehension when Lance mentioned the name *Charles*, whom she knew was really his Uncle Charley. From what Lance had told her about the bad blood between the two men, she wasn't sure getting them together to search her father's files was such a good idea. She glanced over her shoulder at Lance, who smiled and winked. She took this to mean he had thought the problem out ahead of time and had evidently concluded it would work out. She could only hope he knew what he was doing.

It wasn't that Jamie didn't want her father and Charley to work things out. It was, in fact, a great hope on her part. She just wasn't sure this was the best way to go about achieving that hope. She was pretty sure she understood where Lance was coming from. From what he had told her, Ivan and Charley hadn't seen each other in over twenty-five years. *People change in that length of time. The chances of them recognizing each other are pretty slim,* Jamie acknowledged silently. She figured Lance must have been banking that the two of them would hit it off as strangers, and this might help bridge the gap when they were later introduced by their real names. She supposed Lance had an idea of how to keep them from knowing real names for now. He did call his uncle *Charles* instead of *Charley*. She decided to leave this little game in Lance's court and see where it went from there.

CHAPTER 11

Charley opened the door to the motel and took a look around. Living in one motel after another was just a way of life for him. Nothing fancy about this one, but at least it had a kitchenette and that meant some break from restaurant food. Moving to the kitchen, he put the groceries away and opened a can of Sprite. Next he flopped into the overstuffed chair in front of the TV. Using the remote, he flipped it to Channel 3, where the news of a local murder was being reported. Just as he was getting comfortable, he heard the sound of a car pulling into the space in front of his room. He assumed it was a taxi bringing Lance home. He turned to see the young man coming through the door. "I didn't hear a taxi pull away," he observed. "What did you do, rent a car?"

Lance closed the door, then to Charley's surprise, walked straight to the television and switched it off. "What are you doing?" Charley protested. "I was interested in a murder report."

"I know all about the murder, Uncle Charley. I've been right in the middle of the thing."

Charley did a double take. "You've what? Dare I ask how a cop from Orlando got involved in a Mesa murder case?"

"You evidently didn't hear the name of the prime suspect or you might not have to ask that question, Uncle Charley."

Charley took a drink of Sprite. "I might have heard the name of the suspect if someone hadn't shut off my TV. So lay it on me. Who is this mysterious killer?"

"I didn't say he was the killer, Charley. I said he was the prime suspect. As for his name—I think you've heard it before. Ivan Barker."

Charley shot to his feet, knocking over his can of Sprite. "Ivan Barker?!" he bellowed loud enough for the neighbors to hear. "What are you saying, kid?"

Lance moved over next to Charley and picked up the can of soda before all of it spilled. "I'm saying my grandfather is the target of a frame-up," he replied. "I have the proof."

Charley grabbed the soda can from Lance and set it down on the coffee table next to his chair. "Is this some sort of a joke?" he blustered.

Lance grabbed a towel out of the bathroom and tossed it to Charley. "Why would I joke about my own grandfather being called a murderer?" he retorted.

Charley dropped the towel to the spill and used his foot to wipe it up. "I don't like what I'm hearing one bit, Lance Gentry!" he fumed. "Your mother forbid you to ever have a thing to do with that man. Now you're telling me you've gotten yourself mixed up in a police matter concerning him. How could you do this, kid? Your mother wouldn't be happy!"

"My mother wouldn't be happy? What a dumb thing to say."

"There's nothing dumb about honoring your mother's wishes."

"You don't know what you're saying, Charley. I know my mother has forgiven Ivan. You want to know how I know? I know because she came to me in a dream and told me so."

"Dreams don't mean nothing, kid. They're only a wish your heart makes, remember?"

"Not the dream I'm talking about. I saw her, as plainly as I see you right now. She told me she's forgiven my grandfather, and she asked me to forgive him, too."

Charley wasn't buying it. "How'd you happen onto Ivan anyway?" he asked, moving away from the subject of dreams.

"How I met him is a long story, Uncle Charley. I'll tell you all about it when time permits. Right now, we have more pressing matters at hand. I know you're not going to like what I'm about to ask, but I'm going to ask it anyway. I'm building a case to prove my grandfather's innocence. And—I need your help."

"You what?!" Charley spat back. "Forget it, kid! If it concerns Ivan Barker, count me out!"

Lance picked up the towel and folded it. "Look me in the eye and tell me you think my grandfather could be a murderer," he said.

"I never said I thought Ivan was a murderer. Whatever his faults, he's not a murderer."

"So, would you let him take the rap for one without even trying to prove him innocent?"

"Blast you, Lance! You're putting me on a guilt trip, and you know how I hate that! And I wish you'd quit referring to that man as your grandfather."

"He *is* my grandfather, Charley! If you want me to prove it with DNA, I will."

"I don't mean he's not really your grandfather. I mean he's not . . . oh, you know what I mean!"

Lance tossed the towel into the bathroom, then moved over to Charley and put an arm around his shoulder. "Here's the deal, Uncle Charley," he said. "Ivan thinks I'm Lance Smith. He has no idea who I really am. And he doesn't need to know who you are, either. It's been twenty-five years since the two of you have been in the same room together."

Charley's lip turned down into a deep frown, but he didn't answer. Lance went on. "You know the young woman my anonymous benefactor mentioned in the letter, the one he had picked out to help me with my mother's case?"

"Yeah! So what?"

"I met her, Charley. A lovely young woman named Jamie."

"What's that got to do with you sticking your nose into Ivan's case? She was supposed to help with your mother's case."

"I know, Charley. And that's the way things started out. She still will help me with my mother's case just as soon as we're finished with Granddad."

Charley pulled free from Lance and slunk back to the chair. "So how does this young woman tie in with Ivan? Is she a client of his or something?"

Lance moved around until he was standing right over Charley. "Ivan's her father," he bluntly stated.

"What?" Charley shouted, leaping to his feet again. "Ivan has another family now?"

"Just Jamie. He adopted her after Allison died."

Charley grabbed his head in both hands in an attempt to stop the spinning. "Ivan adopted her?" he asked numbly.

"That's right, Uncle Charley. Jamie was ten at the time. She's grown now, and I just met her. She came to me with absolute proof she's the one my benefactor told us about. You know what else, Uncle Charley? Jamie describes Ivan as a much different man from the one you've been telling me about all these years. Don't get me wrong, I'm not disputing your word. What I am saying is, people can change."

Charley lowered his hands as his shoulders slumped forward. "You expect me to believe Ivan Barker's a changed man? That'll take some convincing, let me tell you, kid."

"Fair enough," Lance readily agreed. "And the best way I can think to convince you is by letting you meet the new Ivan, who, by the way, is right outside in Jamie's car."

* * *

Allison shook her head in disgust, listening to her brother's stubborn refusal to do the very thing she knew he had to do if her assignment was to be completed. She knew reaching him wouldn't be easy, even for an experienced angel like she had become over the years, and even being the big sister who had practically raised him. All she could do was give it her best effort. Moving close to Charley, she started speaking to him. "You listen to me, Charley Stapleton. I have some things to tell you, and I expect you to listen. Ivan Barker is my husband, and I love him. He is a changed man, just as Lance is trying to tell you. You're either going to give Ivan the chance to prove himself, or you're going to face the wrath of an irate angel. What'll it be, Charley?"

* * *

Time and again throughout Charley's life, he had the strangest sensation his sister, Allison, was so close he could almost reach out and touch her. To his amazement, the sensation came over him now, and it was almost like Allison was telling him to listen to what Lance was saying. He could almost hear her voice. *You listen to me, little brother. If there's one thing you tried to impress on Lance all through his growing-up years, it was that holding a grudge is wrong. You always told him a grudge is like a little bottle of poison. Those were your very words. You taught him the more he might sip from the bottle, the worse he was going to feel. And you taught him that the person he held the grudge against would never even know about the grudge. How can you expect Lance to ever believe another word you tell him if you aren't willing to live up to your own teaching?*

Charley glanced around the room, almost expecting to see Allison there. The voice seemed that clear.

Something else you need to hear, Charley. Rene has forgiven her father. The dream Lance described was real. She did appear to him. I'm in a position to know. If she's forgiven him, what right do you have not to?

Charley suddenly felt like a ship that had just lost the wind. For the first time, he let himself think about the things Lance was telling him about Ivan's new life. He swallowed his pride and ventured into the subject. "Tell me more about this Jamie," he asked. "What judge in his right mind would have approved a single father to adopt her?"

"All I know is, it happened," Lance answered. "Jamie tells me he had to put up a relentless fight to get the approval."

Charley retreated into some serious thought. "Jamie was ten at the time?" he asked.

"That's right."

"And she says Ivan's been a good father?"

"According to her, he's the best."

Charley's eyes sank into a look of defeat. "Well, maybe he's changed some then. What is it you want from me?"

Lance grinned and patted Charley on the back. "Thanks, Uncle Charley, I knew you'd come through."

"Yeah, yeah, yeah, I'm having a weak moment. You'd better jump on it before I change my mind."

Allison crossed the fingers on both hands. "We have him on the run, Lance. The ball's in your court now, go get him!"

"I've already done a great deal of ground work, Uncle Charley. We're pretty sure the real killer is someone with the initials *SJ*. And we suspect it's someone Granddad sent to prison along the way. What

I'm asking is for you to help him with a file search."

"Looking for someone with the initials *SJ*?"

"Yeah."

Charley exhaled. "Ivan Barker and Charley Stapleton, working side by side doing a file search? How did I let myself get talked into this? You really think you can pass me off as some stranger?"

"Twenty-five years is a long time, Uncle Charley. The only way Ivan's going to know who you are is if you tell him yourself."

"Which you will do if I have any say in the matter," Allison declared.

"Fat chance of that," Charley grumped.

Charley felt trapped but saw no easy way out. Another thought came to mind. "How old is this Jamie?" he asked

"About my age, I'd say," Lance responded. "Why?"

"I don't know, I was just wondering. So, is she a looker?"

"Oh, that's where you're going with this." Lance laughed. "Well, for your information, yes, she is a looker. And if it weren't for the rock I noticed on her left hand, I might like to ask her out sometime myself."

"Rock on her left hand, eh?" Charley couldn't hide his disappointment at hearing this. As far as he was concerned, it was time Lance found someone and settled down. Charley didn't want Lance ending up like him. "So, when do I get to meet the lady with the rock?" he asked. "You said Ivan was outside in her car. Can I assume she's with him?"

"She is. And there's something else you should know before we go outside. Until just this afternoon, Jamie knew nothing about me or my mother. Granddad had kept her in the dark about everything, and he still doesn't know what she's uncovered."

"Humph. It figures the old coot would take that route. I can't say that I blame him. If I was guilty of his sins, I wouldn't want them posted for the world to see, either. Which brings up a question. How did she learn all these things?"

Lance laughed. "I'm glad you asked, Uncle Charley. What she didn't get from me she got from my anonymous benefactor. And get this, he talked with her face-to-face. I have his description, and I think it'll blow you away. I'll tell you all about it when there's time."

"No kidding?" Charley remarked. "The guy is right here

in Mesa?"

"So it seems. And I think he wants us to figure out who he is. So, what about it? Are you ready to go?"

Charley sighed. "Let me throw on a different shirt, kid. This one's got Sprite all over it?"

"Don't wear that green thing with the top button that won't stay fastened," a smiling Allison told him. "I hate that shirt, and it's the one you invariably wear at the most inappropriate times."

The truth was, Allison didn't really care what shirt Charley wore right then. She didn't even care if he wasn't listening. What mattered was he listened when she had more important things to say. She tingled with excitement at thoughts of seeing Ivan and Charley together again, and she knew her assignment was one step closer to a successful conclusion. Satisfied she had things well in hand, she slipped out of the room to rejoin Ivan and Jamie in the Honda.

CHAPTER 12

Allison was about to slip back into the Honda when she paused a moment and stood looking at Jamie. What a beautiful young woman she had become. A tear dampened the corner of Allison's eye as she recognized the outstanding job Ivan had done raising her alone. How many times had Allison wanted to go to Jamie, to caress her and kiss away the hurt of a skinned knee or the pain of harsh words hurled at her by a school-yard bully? How many times had she wanted to fix Jamie's hair "just so" for one of those special occasions when only a mother's tender touch can fill the need? But, just as with Rene, Jamie was never allowed these special "growing up" moments with a mother. Being there as an angel mother was wonderful—for both her girls—but time and time again, Allison had to patiently stand by and watch Ivan play the role of both father and mother—just as she was having to do now with Jamie approaching the threshold of a decision holding eternal consequences. Only this time, Allison did have a voice in the matter. Jamie herself couldn't hear her voice—but Ivan could.

Allison slid through the door into the backseat and flashed a smile at Ivan, who had turned to look at her. "The others will be out in a few minutes," she told him. "In the meantime, there's something I want from you."

Ivan glanced over at Jamie with a questioning look on his face. This brought a laugh from Allison. "What are you worried about, Ivan? You know she can't hear me. But she can hear you, and that brings us to the point of what I want. Remember our little talk about Milton and Lance, and which one was right for Jamie? Sure you do. Well, as her father, it's your place to help her see that Milton's the wrong one. Now I know how hard you try to stay out of Jamie's personal life, and I know your reason for this stems from the mistake you made with Rene. But this time is different. This time you have an angel in your corner making sure you handle things right."

Ivan scowled at her, and she knew what he was thinking. She didn't let up. "Okay," she said. "We need a way to break the ice. Tell you what, you can start by asking her how she met Lance. Yes, that will do nicely for an icebreaker. Go ahead, Ivan. Ask her."

One eyebrow arched as Ivan glanced back and forth between Jamie and Allison. Allison thought for sure it would take more persuasion to get Ivan moving on her plan, but she was delighted when he proved her wrong. "So, Jamie," he asked, with a sincerity Allison was sure rang true, "How did you meet this young Lance?"

"Way to go, Ivan!" Allison shouted out with glee. "I'm proud of you!"

"It's kind of a complicated story, Dad," Jamie responded, her fingers nervously tapping on the steering wheel.

"Not so complicated you can't relate it to your old dad, I hope."

Jamie tried to smile, but it was a short-lived smile that almost instantly fell back to a frown. Allison realized Jamie was struggling with how much to tell her father without revealing what she had uncovered. She was concerned about him being upset. Allison's intent in initiating this conversation was for Ivan to encourage Jamie to listen to her heart about Lance. The conversation had obviously taken a wrong turn and was headed in a completely different direction. All Allison could do now was sit back and see what happened.

"Well, you see, I met Lance through someone else, Dad," Jamie cautiously stated. "I had stopped by the store for pepper. You know, for the dinner I thought you'd be coming to at my place tonight. I know how you love pepper, and I was out."

"Something has you upset, hasn't it, Jamie?" Ivan asked. "I can always tell."

"No, no!" she curtly stated. "You're wrong this time! It's just a complicated story, that's all. When I was leaving the store, this man approached me." She ran a hand through her hair, brushing it away from her face. "He knew I was a P. I., and he wanted to discuss some things with me about opening an old, unsolved murder case. Actually, he only wanted me to help on the case. He explained how this police officer from Florida was already working on it and needed my help because I know my way around Arizona."

"Meaning Lance Smith?" Ivan guessed.

"Yes. This man sent me to Lance's forensic lab. I was there with him, working things out for his case, when you called with the news you'd been arrested. Lance offered to help, and you pretty much know the rest."

Ivan pursed his lips for a moment's thought. "There's one thing I don't know," he offered, "and that's concerning the murder case you and Lance want to reopen. What case is it, Jamie? I'm sure it's one I'd know about if it's local."

"Oh, Dad, it's not a case you need be concerned about. Can we talk about something else?"

"Let it go," Allison remarked. "She doesn't want to talk about it. And you'll be learning all about it from another source very soon now, I promise. Let's get this conversation back on track. Ask her something more personal about Lance. I know, ask her if she thinks he's cute."

"No!" Ivan suddenly stated aloud.

"What?" Jamie asked.

Allison rolled her eyes. "Put your foot in it that time, didn't you, sweetheart? Let's see how you get out of this one."

Ivan cleared his throat. "I just meant no, you don't need my help in the murder case you have on tap. I mean, it looks like you and Lance have everything under control on my case, why not on the other case as well?"

"Oh," Jamie responded, a questioning look still on her face.

"All right, Ivan," Allison spoke up again. "No more fooling around. Ask if she thinks Lance is cute."

Ivan's cheeks puffed as he exhaled a long breath. "I was wondering, Jamie. This Lance . . . do you find him attractive?"

"Daddy! I'm an engaged woman! I'm not supposed to find other men attractive."

"Ask her if she's in love with Milton!" Allison insisted.

Ivan cringed, and Allison knew he was having trouble with this question. She was happy, however, that he didn't let her down. "You know, Jamie, I've never heard you come right out and say how you feel about Milton. I guess what I'm asking is—are you really in love with him?"

"Oh!" Jamie gasped, covering her mouth with her fingers. "Is that the impression I give, that I'm not in love with Milton?"

Allison ignored the pleading in Ivan's eyes. "Don't stop now!" she persisted. "Make her say it one way or the other!"

"I don't mean to judge you, Jamie. But you haven't exactly jumped through hoops setting a marriage date."

Tears suddenly gushed from Jamie's eyes. "That's because I want to be sure, Dad. Surely you can't blame me for that!"

"No," Ivan said, pulling out his handkerchief and handing it to her. "I'm not blaming you for anything. Of course I want you to be sure."

Jamie grabbed the handkerchief and dabbed her eyes. "You think because I offered to help Lance with his investigation I may be having second thoughts about Milton? Is that what you're hinting at?"

Embarrassment filled Ivan's face as this conversation continued to erode. "I didn't say anything like that, Jamie. Let's change the subject, okay?"

"Coward!" Allison scolded.

For a long moment Jamie just sat looking at her father. "All right," she finally agreed, handing back the handkerchief. "But, off the record, do you think Milton is the right one for me?"

Ivan couldn't help it—this last statement brought a laugh he was barely able to stifle. "I think Milton is a great guy. If you love him, marry him. If, on the other hand, you come to the conclusion you don't love him, then wait for the next bus, as the old adage goes."

"She's not in love with Milton!" Allison flatly stated. "She's only fooling herself! You mark my words about that!"

Ivan changed the subject with a question. "What do you know about this Charles that Lance is asking to help with my files? Who is the guy, anyway?"

"Charles is Lance's uncle." Jamie's mouth closed as she realized what she'd just let slip. Allison wondered if Ivan had picked up on it. If so, he didn't show any sign.

The motel door opened and Lance stepped out, followed by Charley. As the men approached the car, Allison held her breath. She had toyed with the idea of telling Ivan who Charley was, but she chose to wait and see how things went first. If Ivan did recognize Charley, not telling him ahead of time could prove to be a mistake. Her mind was put at ease as casual introductions brought no response from Ivan. Allison was proud of Charley's performance, pretending not to know Ivan. Maybe he was a better actor than she thought.

CHAPTER 13

It was an awkward moment for Ivan as he watched Jamie and Lance drive away after dropping off him and a man he knew only as Charles in front of his office complex. Ivan was almost certain Charles was as uncomfortable with this arrangement as he was. The man's handshake had been cordial when they were introduced, but his icy stare almost made Ivan's skin crawl. On the ride from the motel to Ivan's office complex, Charles had taken no part in the conversation. It made Ivan wish he had never come along to help with the search. There was nothing to do now but make the best of a touchy situation. "My office is on the first floor," Ivan explained. "I appreciate the help. This could turn into a lengthy search."

Charley nodded, and the men stepped inside the building. "You have a lovely daughter," Charley said as they made their way toward the office.

"And you have a fine nephew," Ivan said, returning the compliment. "A highly talented young man, I'd say. I'm glad he's in my corner."

Charley stopped abruptly, catching Ivan off guard. "You know Lance is my nephew?" he asked in obvious surprise.

Ivan wondered at the strangeness of this reaction. Was this more of the secret Jamie and Lance had been keeping from him? "Jamie mentioned that you were Lance's uncle. Was she possibly wrong?"

Charley smoothed his moustache nervously as the two men resumed walking. "No, she wasn't wrong. Lance is my nephew. I just didn't realize you knew."

Pushing open the door to his office, Ivan flipped on the light and allowed Charley to step in first. Inside, Charley took a long look. "I'd say you've done well for yourself, Ivan," he observed rather cooly. "This is some office."

"I manage," Ivan answered, doing his best to overlook the curt remark. "I've been at this game a lot of years."

"So you have," Charley observed. "So you have."

Ivan was glad to see Allison had reached the office ahead of them. She was sitting cross-legged on the edge of his desk, wearing a smile that filled her whole face. Ivan marveled at how young and beautiful she looked—much the way she looked that April day in the spring of their lives when they pledged their eternal vows. He wondered if she knew how uncomfortable he was with Charles there. "I know exactly what you're thinking, Ivan," she said, catching his immediate attention. "You're thinking Charley is jealous because you're a successful lawyer."

Ivan straightened and stared at her. Why would she say such a thing? And why would she call the other man *Charley*? "You're wrong, you know," she continued. "It's not that Charley is jealous. His problem runs a lot deeper than mere jealousy."

If Ivan had hoped for sympathy from Allison because of Charles, he was disappointed. What did he care whether or not Charles was jealous? All that mattered to Ivan was getting the job at hand over with so he could send Charles on his way. "I keep my records in those cabinets against that wall," he said, motioning toward the cabinets. "I have files on every client I've ever represented."

Charley glanced as the cabinets. "That's a lot of files," he remarked. "Where do we start?"

Ivan gave it some thought. "I got a look at the killer," he mused. "Offhand, I'd judge him to be in his midfifties. Maybe a little older. It was hard to tell since he was wearing a ski mask. Just for the sake of argument, let's put his age at fifty-five. We're dealing with a lot of variables here, but a good guess would be I sent him to prison at least ten years ago. With that in mind, I'd say we should start looking somewhere around 1990."

Charley threw up both hands. "Why do lawyers always have to complicate things? Let's keep it simple, okay. I'll start looking at your 1980 files and work backward from there. You can start with 1981 and work forward. You got a problem doing it that way?"

Ivan shrugged. "I guess that's as good a plan as any. My 1980 files are over here." Ivan walked to one of the cabinets and opened the top drawer. Charley stepped up behind him and took a look. "Any hints as to how to go about this?" he asked, removing the first file folder from the open drawer.

Ivan reached over and opened the file. "Right here, on the very first sheet," he instructed. "This is an alphabetical listing of anyone involved with this case." He let his finger move down the list to the names starting with *S*. "No one here with the initials *SJ*," he observed. "That eliminates this file. Only a few hundred thousand more to go."

"All the files have this listing in them?" Charley asked.

"Yeah. We at least have that much going for us. I'd hate to think where we'd be without it."

Charley replaced this file and removed the next one in line. As he did, Ivan noticed Allison had stepped up next to him. "I don't know," she offhandedly remarked. "I thought this charade thing would work, but I'm losing faith in it in a hurry."

Ivan had no idea what she was talking about, and what she did next really set him thinking. Moving in even closer to Charles, she actually spoke directly to him. "I've thought it over, Charley, and I've decided it's time to tell Ivan who you really are."

This was a first. Ivan had never seen Allison try speaking to anyone other than him. It was supposedly a rule that only he could hear her voice. He glanced at Charles's face for any indication he had actually heard her. Naturally there was none. But did that stop Allison? No, it didn't. She spoke to him again. "I want you to tell Ivan everything, Charley. It's time he knew."

Ivan was suddenly concerned about himself. Had he allowed this apparition to advance to the point where he could no longer control her at all? Up until now he hadn't worried about it, and since he enjoyed her company, he had taken no steps in looking for a cure. But after this? . . . Ivan considered making an appointment for a session with Frank Levet, one of his clients who happened to be a psychologist.

"I know you're listening to me, Charley," Allison pressed on. "Tell Ivan who you are."

Ivan thought he noticed Charles stiffen, as though he had actually heard Allison and wanted to tune her out. But that was preposterous. He couldn't have heard.

"Darn you, Charley!" Allison scolded. "I know you're listening. Why are you being so stubborn about this? All right. If you won't tell Ivan who you are, I'll tell him myself." She turned to face Ivan. "Take a good look at this man, Ivan. He's older now, but he's still the same Charley you used to slip five dollars to so he would leave you and me alone. He was a kid then, naturally."

Ivan straightened to his full stature and stared at this Charles with renewed interest. "Oh, my!" he gasped as Charles's features began taking on a familiar shape. "Charley Stapleton? It is you, isn't it?"

Charley turned to look Ivan straight in the eye. For a long moment he just stood there. Finally he spoke. "Yeah, I'm Charley. The kids wanted me to keep quiet." There was another lengthy pause as Ivan struggled to comprehend the reality of what he had just learned. "Long time no see," Charley at last remarked.

Ivan felt his heart speed. "Charley Stapleton," he said again. "Where have the years gone?" Then another revelation burst into Ivan's mind. "If you're Charley Stapleton, then Lance must be? . . ."

"You got it, Ivan. Lance is your grandson. And just to clear the air, I had nothing to do with the two of you running into each other. I made a promise twenty-five years ago."

Ivan's eyes lowered. "I know," he replied. "And I never tried to interfere with your keeping that promise."

"So you haven't. I guess I owe you for that."

Allison spoke up. "Charley doesn't know it, but I'm the one who convinced him to help you with your search, Ivan. I wanted to get the two of you together, you know, in hopes you could work things out. It's part of my assignment."

"Lance is my grandson?" Ivan asked again, letting the thought play through his mind. "He's grown into a fine young man. You did a good job raising him, Charley."

"I tried."

"I've always wondered what kind of man he might be today. I never even got to see him as an infant. And before you say it, I know it was all my own fault. It's something that's haunted me every day of my life since it happened." Ivan swallowed away the lump that had formed in his throat. He had always wondered how he might feel if he ever came face-to-face with Lance again, and when the time came, he hadn't even know it was Lance. Finding out now was a shock, but it was a wonderful shock. Ivan couldn't wait for the chance to tell Lance how much he loved him and how proud he was of what Lance had become. As for Charley? Well, there were no words to express his feelings for Charley after the things he had just learned. He brushed a hand through his hair and tried to form the words for his thoughts. "I can't blame you for hating me, Charley. But I want you to know, I'll be eternally grateful for the way you came to Rene's help when she needed you. And for the way you took care of Lance."

Ivan watched as Charley slowly moved to the large window behind Ivan's desk. He stood there nearly a minute, silently staring out into the night. "I wish I could hate you, Ivan," he said, breaking the silence. "But how can I? I raised Lance to respect certain values . . . Honesty. Integrity. Morality. That sort of thing. And way at the top of the list, I taught him the godlike principal of forgiveness." Slowly, Charley turned to face Ivan. "How can I expect Lance to live up to my words if I don't live up to them myself?"

"I did it!" Allison shouted. "I got through that thick skull of yours, little brother! Way to go!"

"You know what your grandson said to me when I rebuked him for not walking away as soon as he realized who you were?" Charley coughed up a halfhearted laugh. "He told me his mother came to him in a dream saying she'd forgiven you. I never put much stock in dreams, but I'm convinced now this one was real."

Once again, Charley was silent for several seconds. Then, after expelling a long breath, he asked, "What do you think, Ivan? Should I forgive you?"

Ivan wet his lips. "How can I ask you to forgive what I can't forgive myself?" he responded. "Let me tell you something, Charley. There's never been a day I wouldn't give my own life to right that wrong. But it doesn't work that way. You can't go back and relive history."

Charley crossed the room to face Ivan again. "I'm not white-washing this. I've resented you, Ivan. I've never entertained the slightest thought of forgiving you. But something is happening to me

I can't explain. It feels like Allison was just here in this very room, telling me I'm wrong."

"I am here," Allison sniffed. "And I'm very proud of you."

"There's something else I want to say while I'm at it," Charley continued. "I always pictured you walking away from the problem like it never happened. I see now I was wrong. You've been punishing yourself for the mistake to the point you've lived in misery. That leaves me feeling a little guilty about keeping your grandson from you."

"I did appreciate the small mementos you sent me along the way," Ivan said. "They meant a lot."

"I didn't send anything, Ivan. Where'd you get that idea?"

This came as a shock to Ivan. Over the years he had received little things in the mail he assumed came from Charley. There were pictures of schools where Lance had supposedly attended, and copies of programs from activities Lance had participated in. Once, there was a baseball Lance supposedly hit out of a high school park for a home run. Granted, these were little things, but they were something Ivan could have to associate with his grandson. If Charley hadn't been the one who sent them, then who could it have been? "I don't understand, Charley. Somebody sent me the stuff."

"Lance's anonymous benefactor," Charley guessed. "I'm betting it was him." Charley shoved both hands in his pants pockets and kicked at the bottom of the nearest cabinet. "Look, Ivan," he struggled. "I'm not saying it's going to be easy. But I'm willing to give our friendship another try. If the idea meets with your approval, that is."

"For Lance's sake, I presume?" Ivan asked.

Charley wiped his mouth. "I admit, that's what motivated me at first. That, and the little voice I mentioned earlier. Bottom line, I want this because I think it can help both of us get past some things. You obviously need to forgive yourself, and I need to forgive you." Charley slowly reached out a hand to Ivan. "What do you say? Want to give it a shot?"

"I'd like that," Ivan agreed as they shook hands. Ivan looked at Allison, who was crying. He wanted to comfort her, but that wasn't easy with Charley here. *Oh, well,* he thought. He was sure the best comfort he could give had already come in the handshake.

* * *

Jamie had learned more about forensic science in the past twenty-four hours than she had learned in all her years as a P. I. They checked fingerprints, blood types, DNA, and the composition of the rubber scraped from Samuel Wagner's garage floor, and then ran everything through elaborate computer programs for a final check.

In the middle of everything else, Lance opened the box of evidence given to him by Sheriff Quinn—the box containing old evidence from his mother's case. An inventory revealed several interesting things. There were samples taken from the point of explosion, where the ransom money mysteriously changed hands. There was a complete autopsy report, including photographs and x-rays of Rene's body. And there were nearly a hundred pages of police reports compiled into a single notebook. Jamie marveled at how well Lance held up as he examined these graphic reminders of his mother's death.

Near the bottom of the box, Lance discovered something of particular interest. There was a small vial containing bits of skin taken from under his mother's nails at the autopsy. Even though they realized at the time that Rene had fought her killer and dug her nails deep into his skin, they had no way of analyzing it in those days. But there was a way now: DNA.

"Are you sure the skin under her nails belonged to the killer?" Jamie asked when she saw what Lance was up to.

"Darn sure," Lance stated. "Mom was strangled. They found her with bloodied nails. It's all here in the report."

Jamie was hesitant to ask her next question, but she felt it was time. "If I'm to be of the most help, Lance, I really should know the whole story of your mother's murder."

Lance stared at the little vial in his hand. "I've already explained I was five. Mom and I were living in an apartment here in Mesa—one belonging to Uncle Charley. He was in and out, constantly checking on us between jobs. The day before the kidnapping, he had finished up a small part in a western being shot in Old Tucson. He drove in that evening in his old Plymouth, figuring to stay a few days before heading on to California to look for more work.

"Most of the time, I rode a bus to my kindergarten class, but that morning Mom borrowed the old Plymouth to drive me there herself. I remember we were just passing the church lot, the one where we attended church on Sundays, when this big black car came up beside us and forced Mom off the road. She ran into a tree at the border of the parking lot."

Jamie felt her skin crawl just thinking about it. "A man pulled us out of our car and forced us into the trunk of his. He slapped me several times because I couldn't stop crying. We were in that dark trunk for a long time."

Lance grew silent for several seconds. Jamie didn't interrupt. "I know Mom had to be scared to death," he at last continued. "She just kept telling me we'd be all right. There was a little song she used to sing to me. It was about a little white duck. She sang it to me over and over while we were in that trunk. To this day, I can hear her voice singing to me. I've never forgotten the words to that song."

Lance removed a handkerchief and wiped his mouth. When he spoke again, there was an obvious tremble in his voice. "When the man opened the trunk I realized we were in the mountains. There was an old log cabin situated near a deep gorge. The man forced us inside and locked us in a room, then he left. I realize now he went to collect the ransom money."

"That was in the White Mountains?" Jamie asked.

"Yeah. The White Mountains. I've since had this confirmed."

"Did you get a look at the guy's face?"

Lance laughed softly. "I thought he was some creature from space. I realize now he was wearing a nylon stocking over his face. To this day, I hate being alone in the dark, and I still have nightmares of his face."

Jamie had no trouble understanding this. She still had nightmares about her mother and father dying in front of her young eyes.

"The room we were locked in had one small window with three iron bars blocking it. Mom tried frantically to get the door open, but it was no use."

Lance set the vial down and turned his attention back to the computer. Jamie wasn't positive, but she thought he was trying to keep her from seeing a dampness in his eyes. "Mom pulled me to her and held me like she wanted to break me in half," he went on. "She was crying so violently I could feel her body quiver. She told me she loved me and that I had to be brave. I had no idea what was going on when she lifted me up to that little window. I remember how it hurt when she forced me out between those cold iron bars. It ripped my clothes and tore the skin off my chest and back, but I made it to the outside. I was terrified."

Jamie felt ill. How could a mother find the courage to do that to her son? But if she hadn't found the courage, Lance wouldn't be here today.

"She told me to run. I was so afraid, I couldn't. I begged her to take me back inside with her. I'll never forget how she looked at that moment. Mom had raven black hair and eyes darker than a midnight sky. She forced a smile, even over her tears. It was a smile warm enough to drive away any monster a five-year-old mind could conceive. 'Run!' she told me again. 'Run and don't stop until you find someone who'll take you home to Uncle Charley. If you see that big, black car again, I want you to hide. But if you see anyone else, I want you to ask them for help. Tell them your name, and tell them to take you to the police.' Mom reached an arm through those bars and stroked my head. She told me whatever happened, she'd always be there with me. Even if I couldn't see her, she said she'd be there.

"I ran down the road a short distance, then turned to see her one last time." Lance could no longer hide his tears, nor could he keep the tremor out of his voice. "She called out to me. She told me she loved me, and she told me to run. That's the last memory I have of her."

Lance pretended to turn his attention back to the computer. Jamie didn't bother him until she could see he was in control again. Only then did she ask her next question. "How did you find your way out of those woods?"

"I did just what my mother said. I ran until I thought I couldn't run another step, then I ran some more. I kept right on running until nighttime fell, then I curled up under a tree and cried myself to sleep. Sometime in the early morning hours, I woke to the sound of a car on the dirt road. I lay close to the ground and watched as the big, black car passed by. I knew the kidnapper was on his way back to Mom. Even the dark couldn't stop me after that. I darted into the woods and kept trudging along all night. I climbed hills, I crossed gullies, I nearly fell over the edge of a canyon, but I just kept going. When morning came I was completely lost. I wandered on aimlessly until I happened onto a little stream, where I got a much-needed drink of water. Not knowing what else to do, I stayed there by the stream, all that day and all through the next night. I was cold and hungry, but I didn't know what else to do. That's when something happened I've never mentioned to another living soul, other than Uncle Charley."

"It's all right, you don't have to tell me if you'd rather not," Jamie remarked.

"I don't mind telling you, Jamie. I'm not sure why, but I really don't mind. When I awoke that morning, I heard my mother's voice calling me. Later reports confirmed my mother was dead by that time. But I know I heard her voice, and it was her instructions that saved my life. Maybe you can see why I'm careful who I tell this to."

"Hey," Jamie said and smiled, "I believe in angels. I know I had one or two very close to me at times when I was a child living in an abusive home. I have no doubt your mother was there for you."

"Nor do I," Lance affirmed. "Her voice guided me over a little hill, where I discovered a mountain road. She prompted me to wait there and promised help would arrive soon. Help did arrive. A man in an old lumber truck found me. He wrapped me in a blanket and drove me to a ranger station."

"Were you ever able to lead the authorities back to the cabin?"

"I was five years old, Jamie. I tried, but I couldn't find my way back. I described it as best as I could remember, and Uncle Charley tells me they made an extensive search, but there's a lot of mountain up there. All I know is it was in the White Mountains because that's where the lumberjack found me. I remember the road leading to the old cabin. It was a steep dirt road with lots of twists and turns, and it was in the middle of heavy pines."

Lance suddenly leaned in for a closer look at the computer screen, where he was comparing some blood samples he had analyzed earlier. "Bingo!" he cried, instantly breaking the mood. "I was right! The blood from the bullet and sofa are a perfect match to the blood on the handkerchief. If we can find our mysterious Mr. *SJ*, we've got the killer!"

"All right!" Jamie exclaimed. "I'll call Dad with the news and see if he's found anything yet!"

"Why bother with a call? Let's drive over there and give them a hand with their search. If Granddad's files are as big as he said, they're going to need all the help they can get."

* * *

Ivan glanced at his watch to see that he and Charley had been working for over an hour on their search. *How strange,* he thought, *it seems like no time has passed at all.* Charley had talked in a steady stream as they worked, filling Ivan in on all the years he had missed seeing Lance grow from a boy to a man. Even Allison hadn't interrupted. She hadn't stopped crying, either. Ivan had to admit, spending this time with Charley was nice. They talked, shared a few laughs, and once Charley even slapped Ivan on the back. It was almost like there had never been a problem between them. Ivan reasoned that this was what real forgiveness should be about.

"I have a question, Charley," Ivan quickly interjected when Charley slowed for a breath. "This old murder case Lance and Jamie are working on together, is it by chance Rene's?"

"Didn't I mention that?" Charley asked. "I didn't even tell you about the anonymous benefactor, did I?"

"I heard you mention a benefactor once, but you didn't explain."

"Well, we can rectify that," Charley grinned.

Ivan was glad to see it was a genuine smile. "Okay, but first, I have one more question. How much does Jamie know?"

Charley paused to look at Ivan. "She knows it all," he said. "And don't you dare jump that young lady out for it, Ivan. She needs to know about her father."

Ivan wanted to respond, but he felt his voice choke. Charley was right. Jamie did have the right to know.

"Let's get back to these files," Charley suggested. "I'll fill you in on that anonymous donor, but first—did I tell you about the time Lance decided he wanted to play the saxophone? I don't know whether you know this or not, but Rene always hated the sax. I tried to talk the kid into taking trumpet instead, but that didn't work out because . . ."

Ivan's eyes were so watery he could hardly see the names on the list in the file he was checking. He noticed Allison was having much the same problem. Returning his attention to Charley, he listened as more of Lance's story flowed like pages from a long-lost book.

CHAPTER 14

Ivan glanced again at his watch, this time to see it was just past midnight. He and Charley had been digging through files for well over two hours, still with no luck. Charley had never slowed in his recounting of the years Ivan had missed out on with Lance. Ivan was especially intrigued by the story of the anonymous benefactor who had paid for Lance's education and had set him up with the lab here in Mesa. Just as Charley was curious about the identity of this man, so was Ivan. Ivan also agreed with Charley's observation about the things Ivan had received from time to time. It only made sense it was this unnamed benefactor who had sent these items.

Eventually, the subject worked around to Charley himself. Ivan wasn't surprised to learn he was still in show business. "Acting's all I know," Charley explained. "I suppose we can't all be doctors or lawyers."

"Don't put yourself down," Ivan argued. "The world needs good actors as much or more than it needs lawyers. And think about it, how many actor jokes do you ever hear?"

"Maybe so, but broken-down actors like me don't make the bucks good lawyers do. And I don't mean that in a bad way. I know you're an honest man, Ivan. You've earned every dime."

"Don't kid yourself, Charley. Real success isn't judged by a bank account. I bet you've lived a happy life as an actor. There have been many times when that wasn't the case with this big-dollar lawyer. The mistakes I made along the way come with a pain that can't be eased by money."

Charley shrugged. "I have lived a happy life," he admitted. "A simple life, and sometimes a lonely life—but happy all the same."

Interrupted by the sound of the door, Ivan turned to see Lance and Jamie just stepping into the room. A lump formed in his throat as he looked at Lance for the first time through a grandfather's eyes. His first instinct was to rush to the young man and bury him in a twenty-five-year-overdue embrace, but this idea withered in a hurry when Charley leaned in close to whisper, "If you have any regard for me at all, don't let Lance know I spilled the beans!" A surge of disappointment gripped Ivan, but he knew he had to respect Charley's wishes. Now that they were friends again, he didn't want to do anything to rock the boat. There would be time enough for repairing bridges when the waters had settled.

"What have you uncovered so far?" Lance asked as he and Jamie approached the two weary searchers.

Ivan tried to answer but discovered his voice refused to work. How could he possibly not have recognized Lance? The young man was every inch Rene's son. The dark hair and eyes, the way he carried himself, even his smile. "The only luck we've had is bad luck," Charley said, coming to Ivan's aid. "I found one *SJ*, but I doubt Sally Jensen is our man. Especially since Sally would be in her nineties now."

Jamie laughed. "I'd have to agree, Charles. Sally doesn't fit the profile."

This idle banter helped Ivan pull himself together. It also helped hearing Jamie use the name *Charles*. Ivan smiled, realizing what was going on here. Everyone felt they had a secret they were keeping from someone else. It was really quite funny.

Again, Jamie spoke. "Lance and I are here to help. Where do you want us to start, Dad?"

"Tell her to check the drawer for 1978," Allison interrupted. "The file you want is in the *October* section." Ivan's eyes shot open, and his jaw dropped. "Don't look at me like that, Ivan," she laughed. "I just figured it was time to move on. And don't worry, I'm not overstepping my bounds. I've been given permission to help out this time."

Part of Ivan wanted to laugh this off as just a trick of his mind, but another part rationalized it was worth checking. He didn't say a word to Jamie, but went straight to the file drawer himself. There was only one folder under that exact date. He pulled it out and opened it up to the shock of his life. The name was right there on the very top line. "Sylvester Jarvis!" he numbly stated. "I've found him."

The other three in the room exchanged curious glances. It was Jamie who dared voice what they were all thinking. "How did you do that, Dad? Out of all these files, how did you walk straight to that one?"

Allison laughed. "Let's see how you get out of this one, my dear, sweet husband."

Ivan suddenly felt very foolish. How could he explain? "I'm not sure." He shrugged. "It was like a little voice whispering in my ear." He studied the file more closely. "I remember now! My gosh, has it really been that long since I sent this guy away? How could I ever forget Sylvester Jarvis? They led him out of the courtroom yelling obscenities and threatening my life. Not a pleasant experience, let me tell you."

Lance stepped up and took the file from Ivan. "This one adds up," he said, searching through the pages for himself. "It says here that a highway patrolman spotted Sylvester in a stolen car and attempted to pull him over. Sylvester made a run for it and a high speed chase ensued. It ended with Sylvester crashing into a light pole when he failed to make a turn. And get this, the guy had a warrant out for his arrest. He was wanted on a murder charge, the same charge you eventually prosecuted him for."

"Jarvis killed a man in a barroom argument," Ivan cut in. "He'd been on the run for more than two years when they caught him. Getting the jury to convict the guy was a cakewalk."

"Maybe so," Lance observed. "But you didn't get the death penalty you went after."

"Yeah, Judge Lloyd Gates tried that case. Gates never handed down a death sentence. The best I could do with Jarvis was twenty years to life."

"Twenty years to life?" Jamie questioned. "That would make him eligible for parole around 1999."

"So it would," Lance concurred. "I'm betting our Mr. Jarvis got his parole. Can you get your friend the sheriff to check this out, Jamie?"

"I'll give him a call first thing in the morning. I agree—if Jarvis was paroled, he is the guy we're looking for." She walked up to her father and straightened his collar. "How did the two of you pass your time, other than looking through all these boring files?" she asked.

Ivan stifled a smile, realizing his daughter was digging for information. For the first time he realized he wasn't angry, hurt, or anything else because she discovered things he had kept hidden all these years. In fact, he was glad she at last knew. But he sort of liked the idea that she didn't know what he knew. He decided to make the most of it. After a quick wink at Charley, he said, "Charles and I had a very nice conversation, Jamie. It seems he's an actor. Did you know that?"

Jamie and Lance exchanged glances. "Lance mentioned it to me, yes," she answered, fidgeting with the strap on her purse.

"He used to live here in Mesa. Way back when. Small world, isn't it?" The looks on Jamie's and Lance's faces made it all the harder for Ivan to hold back the laugh waiting to escape his throat.

"He lived in Mesa? That's nice, Dad."

Tempting as it was to keep this fun little game going, Ivan realized the lateness of the hour. "Maybe we should call it a night," he observed. "We've done about all the good we can for one day, and I'm sure we could all use some rest."

Ivan and Charley were the last two out of the room. Just before stepping through the door, Charley leaned over and whispered, "You were having entirely too much fun back there, Ivan, and I loved every second of it. When shall we tell the kids we're onto them?"

"Let's just play it by ear," Ivan whispered back.

As Ivan went to turn out the light, he noticed Allison was right behind him. She was smiling and crying at the same time. Ivan had never seen her looking more beautiful. He felt a sudden urge to talk with her. "Oh, I forgot something, Charley," he quickly said. "There's something I need to get from my desk. You run on with the others. Tell them I'll be right there."

As soon as Charley stepped away, Ivan closed the door and faced his wife. "I have no idea how you directed me to the right file," he told her. "I'm completely baffled."

"I'm an angel, Ivan. I can do things like that if the authorities approve it."

Ivan did something he had never done before. He reached out and touched the point where it appeared her cheek should be. Of course he felt nothing. "I'm sorry, Ivan," she said, realizing his disappointment.

"Another angel rule?" he asked.

"Something like that. But I am real."

"Oh, Allison, you have no idea how badly I want you to be real. You're so good for me." He withdrew his hand. "Even as a made-up ghost, you're good for me. I hope you never go away."

Allison's smile was still there, but now it didn't reach her eyes. "I can't stay here forever," she said. "Not like this. Once my assignment is finished, things will go back to the way they were before. I'll still be here, but you won't be able to see me or talk with me. I'll just be a little voice in your heart, like I was with Charley tonight."

"I don't want you to go away, Allison."

"I'm sorry, Ivan, but it's the way things have to be. Just remember, we will be together again when the time comes."

"When the time comes?" he echoed. "And when will that be?"

"Angels don't have a crystal ball, Ivan. I don't know when you'll join me, but I do know I'll be here waiting when the time comes."

"Promise me you'll stay the night with me," he pleaded.

This time, her smile was complete. "I promise, Ivan. I'll stay this night with you."

Something in the way she said it left Ivan wondering if this would be the last night she'd stay with him. He was too frightened of the answer to press the question.

"I can tell you this much," Allison calmly stated. "Tomorrow is going to be a big day. I suggest you join the others so you can get home for some sleep."

After one last look at his beautiful wife, Ivan flipped off the light and stepped out the door, closing it behind him.

CHAPTER 15

Long after Ivan had dropped off to sleep, Allison remained at the foot of his bed just looking at him. In a way, she wished she hadn't mentioned that she might soon be leaving him again, but it really wouldn't be fair to simply vanish without a word. She realized her assignment here was nearly complete, and once it was, it would mark the end of this personal contact she had enjoyed these few weeks. Ivan wasn't the only one who wished it didn't have to end.

Moving to the edge of his bed, she leaned down and placed an angel kiss on his cheek. "We're going to be a real forever family, you know," she whispered. "You, me, Rene, Jamie, Neil, Lance, Charley, all of us. The only thing left standing in our way is your self-inflicted guilt. We're all required to forgive, and that includes forgiving ourselves. I have to convince you of that before I leave, and there's not much time. Speaking of which, there's another area of my assignment that needs taking care of right now. Sleep on, my dear husband. And dream of me."

One advantage to being an angel was the ability to move from place to place in the twinkling of an eye. As a newcomer angel, this had been especially thrilling for Allison, and it had required some getting used to. By now she was an old hand at it, and so it was only second nature for her to leave Ivan's side and be with Jamie in less than a heartbeat.

How many times over the years had Allison admired Jamie while she slept? And how many times had she whispered *I love you* to her sleeping child? Moving to her side now, Allison sat on the bed and leaned in close. "I have some things to tell you, Jamie," she whispered. "I want you to listen very carefully tonight. You know I've been telling you for some time how Milton isn't the right one. That's why I've worked so hard to convince you to keep putting off the date. Well, I have some great news. The one I promised would be coming along is here. His name is Lance Gentry."

A smile crossed Jamie's face, a sigh escaped her lips, and she rolled onto her back. "You know I'm telling the truth, don't you?" Allison continued.

Jamie sighed again and breathed the name *Lance*.

Allison laughed and moved on to another pressing matter. "I want you to think back, Jamie. To your eighteenth birthday. You may not realize this when you're awake, but in your sleep I'm sure you remember I was the one who put the idea in your mind to ask for a daddy-daughter outing as your present that year. I want you to remember that daddy-daughter outing now. Just relax and dream about it as I relate it to you in fine detail. And tomorrow, I want you to remember the dream, Jamie. Your very future depends on it."

CHAPTER 16

Jamie felt the warmth on her face before opening her eyes to see it was caused by a stream of sunlight penetrating the blinds and forming a halo around her pillow. "Oh, no," she groaned. "It can't be morning already." Suddenly, she shot up in bed, eyes wide open as the dream she had just awakened from played out vividly in her mind. "Oh my!" she called out. "Is it possible?" Then, glancing at the clock, she realized it was after ten. How could she have allowed herself to sleep so late when there was so much to be done? Scrambling out of bed, she threw on a housecoat, grabbed the phone, and punched in the numbers for Sheriff Quinn's office. The sheriff himself answered.

"Sheriff, this is Jamie Barker. I need a favor."

"You want me to put out a search to see if Sylvester Jarvis has been paroled?" Quinn responded with a low, rolling chuckle. "Your dad called an hour ago."

"Dad already called?" she asked sleepily.

"Yeah. I have a man on it now, and I should have an answer within the hour. By the way, digging out Jarvis's name was a great piece of detective work. I'm impressed."

"Have someone call me as soon as you hear, okay? I'll have my cell phone on."

"Will do, Jamie. That's a promise."

Jamie had to laugh at herself for letting her dad upstage her this way. He might have been growing old, but it certainly wasn't slowing him down. He wasn't the one who overslept with so much work to be done. "Thanks, Sheriff," she said. "You're a sweetheart."

Jamie cleared the line and hurriedly placed a second call, this time to Lance's motel. She got Charley. "This is Jamie," she told him. "Is Lance there by chance?"

"No, the kid was up at the crack of dawn. Said he had some catching up to do at the lab."

Jamie cringed. Now she'd been upstaged twice. "Thanks, Charley. I'll give him a call."

"Listen, kid—before you hang up . . ."

"Yes?"

"I take it Lance filled you in on my opinion of Ivan—your father . . ."

"He did."

"Well, just let me say—after seeing Ivan again and working with him on those files last night . . .What I'm trying to say is, I may have been wrong. It appears to me that Ivan may be a changed man. And, I'd like to add, I think he did a bang-up job raising you, Jamie. You strike me as a very special young woman."

"Thank you, Charley. That's very kind."

"Well, anyway, you can probably catch Lance on his cell phone. Like I say, he's at the lab."

Jamie was pleased that Charley and her dad had gotten along so well. As she placed the phone back on the hook, more thoughts of last night's dream emerged. She had dreamed of the day she and her father rode up into the White Mountains on horseback. It was on her eighteenth birthday. Funny how she had completely forgotten about that old log cabin they saw until the dream reminded her. She reasoned it was Lance mentioning a log cabin that triggered the dream in the first place. The chances of it being the same cabin where he and his mother were held captive were slim, but she'd mention it to him anyway. It couldn't hurt.

She picked up the phone again, this time with the intention of calling Lance. As she did, she suddenly realized she was humming a tune she'd heard on the radio as she and Lance drove to police head-quarters to pick up her dad yesterday. She also realized just how pleasant it had been spending the day with Lance. She even felt a hint of excitement at the prospect of hearing his voice on the other end of the phone now. What was the matter with her? She certainly couldn't let Milton learn how giddy she was acting around another man. She forced these thoughts from her mind and made the call.

"Hello?"

"Lance?"

"Jamie? I was hoping you'd call. I have some news. The bits of skin taken from beneath my mom's fingernails contain a strong DNA signature. I'm running tests to break it down now."

"That's great!" Jamie responded. "I have something to tell you, too. Will you be at the lab awhile?"

"Should be. I have mounds of evidence to sort out."

"Let me grab a quick shower, and I'll be right over. I hate to admit this, but I slept longer than I intended."

"When do you figure on being here?"

"Let's make it an hour, okay? That should give me ample time."

"An hour it is. I'll have lunch waiting. There's a little sandwich shop just down the street. How does a French dip sound?"

"Sounds yummy! I love French dips. See you in an hour."

All through her shower Jamie couldn't stop thinking of her dream. The possibility of it aiding in Rene's murder case continued to increase in her mind to the point that she felt compelled to act. She determined that one more call to Sheriff Quinn was in order before leaving the house.

Jamie pulled into the lot and parked her car just in time to see Lance returning from the sandwich shop with their lunch. She rushed to help with some of it so his hands would be free to get the door. "Good morning." He grinned. "And thanks for the help. I was wondering how I was going to manage the door."

"This smells great," Jamie remarked. "I must be hungrier than I realized."

Inside, they pulled lab stools up to one of the tables. "One French dip and an order of fries for you," Lance said, pulling them out of the bag and placing them down in front of her. "And one root beer. I hope you like root beer. I didn't ask."

"Root beer's fine." She smiled and watched as he removed a French dip and fries out of the sack for himself.

"So?" Lance began as they settled on their stools, "What was it you wanted to tell me?"

Jamie popped the top off her au jus. "Before I tell you, you have to promise not to laugh," she said.

Lance took a bite of a french fry and glanced questioningly over at her. "You don't want me to laugh?"

"What I want to tell you might seem goofy, but it could also prove to be important. No laughing at me, okay?"

"Okay, I won't laugh. So, what's the deal?"

"The deal is, I had a dream last night. I dreamed about my Dad's birthday present to me when I turned eighteen."

"A dream?" Lance questioned.

"Just hear me out, okay? I have this thing about horses. I've always loved them. And I love riding. So for my birthday, Dad rented a pair, and the two of us spent the day riding in the White Mountains."

"The White Mountains?" Lance asked, his interest suddenly piqued. "Go on! I'm listening."

"While we were out that day, we happened onto an old log cabin. I'd forgotten about it until my dream last night. I know there are a lot of cabins in those mountains, but the one you described sure sounds like the one Dad and I saw that day. It was situated next to a deep gorge, just like the one in your story."

If Jamie was worried about Lance laughing, she could see now that she could put the idea to rest. His eyes were bursting with anticipation. "Could you find the place again?"

She dipped her sandwich into the au jus. "Are you saying you'd like for me to find it again?"

"Yeah, I would! If there's a chance it's the same cabin, I'd like to have a look at the place."

Jamie took a bite of sandwich and made him wait until she finished chewing. "I thought you might feel that way," she said. "I was so sure, I've even arranged transportation up to the place."

"What?" He laughed.

"I called Sheriff Quinn and explained the thing about the cabins—all except for my dream. I left that part out. But I told him about the cabin Dad and I saw and about the cabin you described. He was interested enough to make the department's helicopter available to us."

"Quinn's loaning us a helicopter? When?"

"As soon as I call him back and tell him we're ready. Which I'll do when I finish this sandwich, but not one bite before. This is too good to put down."

"You're serious? There's a chopper waiting to take us up to the cabin now?"

"Can I take it you want me to make the call?"

"You're darn right I do. No one ever figured out how the kidnapper made off with the ransom money without being seen. If your cabin does turn out to be the right one, who knows what secrets it might reveal?"

"Even after twenty-five years?" she asked.

"You never know what might have survived, Jamie. Remember the old saying 'what if walls could talk?' Well, with today's forensic technology, walls often *can* talk."

"I want to hear the story of how the kidnapper got the ransom money," Jamie remarked.

"Eat your sandwich, then make that call. I'll tell you all about it on the flight up to the cabin."

Behind them, an unseen angel smiled at how well her plan was coming together.

CHAPTER 17

Ivan stepped into Sheriff Quinn's office to see him on the phone. Quinn spotted Ivan and motioned him over to the desk. "Yeah, Ralph," Quinn spoke into the phone. "Two months ago yesterday. And you say he never checked in with his probation officer?"

Ivan didn't like the sound of this one bit. Putting two and two together, he could only assume Quinn was talking to someone about Sylvester Jarvis's probation. Ivan had called ahead to get Quinn moving on the matter before he started over there.

"Thanks, Ralph," Quinn said, ending the conversation and dropping the phone on the hook. "You were right, Ivan. Jarvis was paroled two months ago. The worst of it is, he's never checked in with his parole officer. We have no idea of his whereabouts."

Ivan exhaled loudly. "Looks like he's our man then, doesn't it?"

"I want you in protective custody, Ivan. I was in the courtroom the day that maniac threatened to kill you. That guy's as bad as they come. I don't want you out there with a target painted on your back."

Ivan shook off the idea. "If Jarvis wanted to kill me outright he could have done it at Wagner's house. This guy wants to make me suffer, Quinn. He probably wants me in prison, where I had him committed for twenty-plus years. Protective custody is out. I have things to do."

"Even if what you say is true, Ivan, the guy's going to have second thoughts when he realizes he failed to frame you for Wagner's murder. I want you where I can keep an eye on you."

"How's he going to find out the frame-up failed? We can keep it under wraps for a while, probably long enough to bring him in."

"And what charge am I going to hold him on?"

"Parole violation," Ivan shot back. "That'll keep him off the streets until we can come up with something better. I appreciate what you're trying to do, Sheriff, but I have my reasons for not wanting to be locked up. I just came across some information that's going to change my life, and I need my freedom to work some things out. Now get me a release order on my car. You won't be needing it for evidence anymore."

The sheriff shook his head dejectedly. "You're sure about this?" he asked in one last-ditch attempt.

"I'm sure," Ivan retorted. "So what about my car? Do I get it?"

Taking a form from a rack atop his desk, Quinn wrote out the release order and handed it to Ivan. "I want your word you'll keep your cell phone on," he instructed. "You sometimes forget, you know."

Ivan grinned. "You have to understand, old friend. Cell phones are strange new gadgets in the arsenal of an old warrior like me."

"Maybe so, but a slingshot was a strange new gadget to Goliath, too, and look where it got him. I want you available, just in case. Keep that phone on, you hear me?"

"I'll keep it on."

"There's one other thing you should know about Jarvis. The man's an arms expert. He learned it from his years in the army, back in the sixties. All the more reason for you to consider him dangerous."

Ivan stood and walked to the door. "I'll watch myself, Sheriff. I promise."

"You want me to call Jamie with the news or do you want to do it?"

"I'll call her, Quinn. Just as soon as I check on my car."

Leaving the office, Ivan headed straight for the compound where he knew they had taken his Lexus. Once there, he approached the desk where officer Don Murphy was on duty. "I'm here for my car, Don," he told the officer. "Here's the release order."

Don took the release order and told Ivan to grab a chair while he went to the back to check on the car. Instead of sitting down, Ivan moved over to look at a picture hanging on the wall behind the desk. Ivan had seen the picture many times before. It was a picture of a group of officers who had served on the force some twenty or more years ago. The only one out of the group left on the force today was Sheriff Quinn. "He sure looks young in that picture, doesn't he, Ivan?" Allison, who had just shown up, remarked. "Where have all the years gone?"

Ivan glanced over his shoulder at her. "Where have you been?" he asked. "I haven't seen you all morning."

"I have other people to look after besides just you, Ivan. I'm a very busy angel, whether you know it or not."

Ivan looked back at the picture. "It has been a lot of years since this was taken," he observed. "But you and Rene were both gone even back then. Believe me, Allison, living a long life isn't all it's cracked up to be. Maybe you were the lucky one after all."

"What's this?" Allison rebuked. "You're having a pity party? What brought this on?"

"I don't know. It's just sad, my meeting Lance this way. He's all grown now, Allison. And I never got to watch one day of it."

"No, you didn't, did you?" Allison replied. "This isn't a perfect world, Ivan. No one gets through it without stepping on a few thorns along the way. But look at it this way, you've met Lance now. And you'll soon be dancing at his wedding. His and Jamie's."

"Are you sure about that, Allison? Milton seems so perfect for Jamie."

"Just like Robert Cranston was so perfect for Rene?"

Ivan flinched. "Okay, I get your point. But it seems a little strange having a matchup between my grandson and my daughter."

"Stop it, Ivan! You know perfectly well Jamie and Lance are not biologically related."

"I know, but it still seems strange." Ivan released a long sigh. "I wonder when I'll be able to tell Lance I know who he is?"

"It won't be long, dear. Take my word for it."

"I'm afraid I have some bad news," Officer Murphy said, stepping back in the room. "It seems we've temporarily misplaced your car."

"You've what?" Ivan barked. "You impounded my car, and now you've misplaced it? That's preposterous!"

Murphy pointed to a line on his inventory list. "Our records show your car is here at the compound, but we can't locate it at the moment. I don't know what to say. My hands are tied. I'll keep checking and let you know as soon as anything turns up."

"Oh, wonderful, you'll let me know if it turns up. And what am I supposed to do for a car in the meantime?"

"I'm sorry, Mr. Barker, we don't provide loaners. I will initiate a search for your car, but that's all I can do."

Ivan threw up both hands. "I don't believe this! What kind of department are you running here, Murphy? How could you lose my car?"

"Calm down, Ivan," Allison cut in. "It's just a little thing. They'll find your car. Have the officer call you a taxi. You can go straight to a rental lot and get something to use in the meantime."

Ivan removed his glasses and rubbed his eyes. Allison was right, as always. A misplaced car wasn't anything to get his ulcer aggravated over. "All right, officer," he said, lowering his voice. "Since I don't have the number of a cab company, I'd appreciate your calling one for me. Have them pick me up out front, okay?"

"Will do, Ivan. And we will find your car, I promise."

CHAPTER 18

Jamie had just taken a bite of her sandwich when her cell phone rang. Hurriedly she swallowed the bite while digging the phone out of her purse. "This is probably Sheriff Quinn," she told Lance. "He's supposed to call me when he learns something about Sylvester Jarvis being paroled." She pressed the receive button. "Hello?"

"Hi, Jamie, it's me."

"Dad? Oh, I thought it might be Sheriff Quinn."

"I just left Quinn's office. We were right—Jarvis was paroled two months ago."

"Jarvis was paroled," Jamie said to Lance, repeating the information. "Two months ago."

Lance nodded as Jamie went back to her phone conversation. Ivan continued. "There's one more thing, Jamie. Jarvis hasn't reported in since getting out. They don't know where he is."

"Oh, Daddy! That puts you in danger!"

"Don't you start on me, Jamie. I already had a fight with Quinn. He wanted to put me in protective custody."

"That's where you belong, Dad! You can be so stubborn at times!"

"That's my right. I'm old enough that I've earned it. So what's going on at your end? Anything new?"

"Yes, a couple of things. Lance has dug up a DNA sample on a killer he and I have been trying to track down. You know, the one in the special case I mentioned we're working on. Lance is running a workup on it now."

"Are you kidding me? Lance has DNA on Re—" Ivan stopped midsentence to clear his throat, then went on to say, "That is, he's found DNA on a killer you were looking for?"

Jamie pulled back the phone and stared at it. Had she imagined it, or had Ivan started to say Rene's name? Was there a chance he might have guessed? But how could he have? She must have imagined it. "Believe it or not, Daddy, the evidence for this old murder has been sitting in a box of evidence in Sheriff Quinn's care for a lot of years. It took Lance to find it. Something else too. Do you remember that cabin we saw in the mountains the day we rode the horses up there on my eighteenth birthday?"

"Vaguely. What about it?"

"We've discovered the cabin might have something to do with the same case," she explained. Sheriff Quinn is lending us the department's helicopter. We're going up to the cabin for a look-see. Who knows what we might find!"

* * *

Ivan covered the mouthpiece of his phone and turned to Allison. "I need to know something," he pressed. "When Rene was kidnapped, was there a mountain cabin involved?"

"Yes," Allison confirmed. "That's where the kidnapper took her while he retrieved the ransom."

Ivan wet his lips. "I didn't know."

Allison continued. "It never really came out in the investigation. All they had to go on was the word of a five-year-old boy, so they didn't check it as thoroughly as they should have."

Ivan continued to cover the phone as he responded. "That five-year-old boy has grown up now, Allison. He and Jamie are talking about checking out an old cabin she and I saw on an outing we shared some time back."

"On Jamie's eighteenth birthday. I was there, Ivan."

Ivan nodded and reasoned to himself that this might be a good time to reveal some things he had been keeping from Jamie. "Let me ask a question," he said to her. "This mountain cabin you're talking about, was it possibly part of a kidnapping case at some time in the past?"

* * *

Jamie caught a quick breath. Her dad was obviously at the point of figuring things out that she wasn't comfortable with him knowing just yet. She figured it was time for a hasty retreat. "I'm not exactly sure about that, Dad, but I really should be going now. Lots to do before the chopper picks us up, you know."

"Wait, Jamie!" Ivan shouted. "Don't hang up!"

Jamie tossed a worried look at Lance and mouthed the words, *He's getting close to figuring things out.*

"So, let him," Lance whispered back. "You can't keep him in the dark forever."

"I'm still here, Dad," she said, hoping he didn't detect the anxiety in her voice.

"Listen, Jamie. I'm aware of just about every old, unsolved case there is in these parts. The only one that comes to mind involving a kidnapping is one that makes me wonder if you've been doing some digging where I've never wanted you to. You know about Rene, don't you?"

The statement shocked her. *He knows,* she mouthed to Lance, who only smiled and took a bite of his sandwich. "All right, Daddy," she sheepishly admitted. "I know about Rene. Don't be too angry. I uncovered it by accident, not by digging into your past."

She held her breath, waiting for his next remark. Her fears were soon put to rest. "It's all right, Jamie. I'm glad you know. I should have told you years ago."

"Thank you, Daddy," she said softly. She hesitated a moment, then switched to an offense of her own. "But how do you think it makes me feel learning I have a sister you've never told me about? Maybe I have the right to be a little angry myself!"

Jamie heard him sigh. "Believe me, Jamie, I had my reasons."

"I know you had your reasons," she sniffed. "I'm not angry, but it does come as a shock."

Jamie reasoned if Ivan hadn't already figured out the truth about Lance and Charley, it wouldn't be long in coming. She decided not to bring up the subject. It would be better for him and Lance to come together as grandfather and grandson in person rather than over the phone anyway.

"My taxi's here. I need to run."

"Taxi? That's right, you never got your car out of impound, did you?"

Ivan laughed. "There's more to that story than you know, but I'll have to tell you later."

"Dad! I just want you to know that . . . I just want you to know I love you."

"I love you, too. We'll talk more as soon as time permits, okay?"

"Okay, Dad."

"I take it he's figured part of it out," Lance said as she hung up the phone. "Did he mention anything about—you know?"

"No. But I'm sure he'll figure it out pretty soon now." Jamie glanced at her watch. "I'd better make that call to Sheriff Quinn so he can send the chopper out."

"Send it out?" Lance asked. "It's picking us up here?"

"In the parking lot. The sheriff assured me there's plenty of room for it to land."

Lance jumped up. "I need to throw some equipment together, just in case."

CHAPTER 19

"There it is, Pat," Jamie told the chopper pilot, pointing out a log cabin in a small clearing just ahead of them. "There should be plenty of room to set down in the meadow just to the east of the place."

"Plenty of room," Pat concurred. "I've put this baby down in a lot smaller places than this."

Jamie looked over at Lance, whose attention was fixed on the cabin. "What do you think?" she asked. "Could this be the place?"

"I'd almost swear to it, Jamie. I'll know for sure when we see it from the ground."

"You have to admit, it does fit your description. Right down to the deep gorge on the west side."

"Yeah. Even the road leading to the place fits."

"Hang on," Pat called back to them. "I'll have you on solid earth in less than a minute."

Jamie loved flying of any kind, but she found flying in a chopper to be the most fun of all. She likened it to the hummingbird which, she always reasoned, mastered the skies better than any of its winged cousins—in spite of its size. She stared at the ground as the chopper hovered over the meadow then floated ever so gently down to earth. Pat cut the engine and the noisy propellers coasted to a stop.

Lance was the first one to climb out. Dropping his bag of equipment, he turned and helped Jamie down. He offered a hand to Pat, but she declined. "I'll stay here with the bird," she suggested. "You guys go on and do your detective work."

Jamie's eyes remained glued to Lance's face as he got his first close-up look at the cabin. She knew his thoughts instantly, even before he spoke. "This is it!" he cried. "I'm positive, Jamie!" He grabbed his bag. "Come on, let's check it out."

Seeing the cabin again left Jamie amazed at how precise her dream had been, right down to the tiniest detail. "What do you really expect to find after all these years?" she asked as they moved in closer.

"I'm not sure. But if I've learned one thing from my profession, it's never good to rule out a lead, no matter how small."

The cabin was really in pretty good shape considering its age. The roof had a few holes, and part of the rock chimney had fallen away, but that was to be expected. The front door was also missing, as was the glass in the two windows visible from the front. Lance suddenly stopped, and Jamie realized he was looking at one of the windows. It was the smaller one, to right of the door. A shudder passed through her as she noticed three iron bars placed vertically over the opening of this one, and she realized it must be the window Lance said his mother forced him through in order to save his life. Jamie saw the pain in Lance's eyes, and she could only guess what he must have been feeling. It was through this very window he last saw his mother. For several seconds he stared, then, brushing a hand across his forehead, he turned his attention to the doorway. Removing a six-cell flashlight from his bag, he stepped to the opening.

Jamie moved up behind him to look for herself. A substantial amount of light entered the room through the door and window, but Lance used the strong beam of his flashlight to check the more shaded areas. Jamie could see the room was empty of furniture and was blanketed with a thick layer of gray dust. Cobwebs hung in abundance from every corner and crevice in the room, including the fireplace opening. It made her skin crawl.

She watched as Lance knelt down to examine the floor. "What are you doing?" she jested. "Looking for termite damage?"

"Footprints," he responded. "They're barely noticeable, but they are footprints. Probably not more than a few weeks old."

Jamie couldn't help but wonder why Lance would be interested in these footprints. True, this cabin was in an isolated area, but that wouldn't keep an occasional visitor from stumbling onto it. After all, she and her father had done just that the day they were riding in these mountains.

Lance pulled out his camera and took a few shots of the prints. "It was a man," he explained. "A size eleven shoe, I'd guess." Jamie grinned to herself, thinking of some of the shoes the younger generation of girls were wearing these days. It was one point her scientific friend just might have overlooked in assuming the prints were made by a man.

Lance explained his theory as he slipped on another set of latex gloves. "These prints probably don't mean much, but my training tells me to look at everything. Too much evidence is better than not enough."

He handed her a set of gloves, then used his flashlight to brush the cobwebs from the doorway. Slowly, he inched forward, carefully examining the path in front of him before taking a step. Jamie followed, making sure to duck low enough to clear the cobwebs. She did a mental evaluation of the place. There was no running water or electricity. There appeared to be only two rooms. The one they were in was the largest and it contained the fireplace. She could see inside the second room through an open door which, unbelievably, still hung on its hinges. The second room was smaller, and she was aware it was the one with the barred window. She guessed the cabin was probably built by some outdoorsman who long ago had come to these mountains to hunt and fish. She had no idea why there were bars on the window and wondered if they might have been put there by the kidnapper himself.

She followed along as Lance moved to the fireplace. He pointed his light at something on the floor, which she quickly recognized as an old briefcase. "What do we have here?" Lance muttered as he stooped for a closer look. "The amount of dust on this case isn't consistent with the rest of the room," he observed. "That tells me it hasn't been lying in this spot all that long."

Jamie considered this. "What do think of this idea?" she asked. "Whoever those footprints belong to dropped the case there."

"I'd say that's a pretty good assumption. Judging from the thickness of dust on the case, the time frame is about right." Lance removed a small brush from his bag of equipment, which he used to dust off the top of the briefcase. "Would you look at this!" he exclaimed. "We have a name tag with the initials *IB* engraved on it."

"*IB*?" Jamie blurted out. "You're not thinking that briefcase belonged to my dad, are you?"

"I'm not sure what to think, Jamie. From the stories Uncle Charley has told me, Granddad paid the ransom money in a brief-case. And his initials are *IB*. We can't rule anything out."

"Lance! It's been twenty-five years! How could Dad's briefcase have remained in this old cabin all that time? That's unreal!"

"I don't have any answers right now, Jamie. But strange things happen in cases like this. We can't rule out that this might be the briefcase Granddad paid the ransom in. It is pretty timeworn, as you can see."

"I don't know, Lance. It takes a pretty big stretch of the imagination to think that could be the same briefcase."

"Yeah, well, I think I'll take it back to my lab and check it out all the same." Lance removed a large plastic bag from his equipment pouch and placed the briefcase inside it. While Lance was busy with this, something on the fireplace hearth caught Jamie's eye. The hearth was constructed of red brick with a layer of flagstone atop it. She noticed one large piece of flagstone had been moved aside. What caught her eye was the hollowed-out compartment beneath the missing flagstone. It suddenly struck her that an object the size of this briefcase might fit in that compartment, and if the flagstone were placed over it—it might well go undetected.

"Lance," she said, "what if that briefcase had been hidden from view all these years?" He looked up as she pointed to what she had found. "Maybe it isn't such a stretch of the imagination after all," she admitted. "What do you think?"

Lance moved to the hearth and shined the flashlight into the hollowed-out compartment. "You're on to something, Jamie. That briefcase has been in this compartment. Bits of leather have pulled loose and have adhered to the stone at the bottom." Lance quickly leaned down and scraped a sample of the leather from the stone, which he put in a small plastic bag. "I'll check for sure, but there's little doubt this came from that briefcase."

Lance turned his attention to the piece of flagstone that had been removed, revealing the hidden compartment. "The thickness of dust on this stone matches that on the briefcase," he stated. "I see a picture developing here, Jamie. Someone's been in this cabin recently. They found where the briefcase was hidden and removed it."

Jamie watched as Lance used a little air blower to remove the dust from the loose flagstone. Once this was done, he pulled out an aerosol can and sprayed it. To her amazement, several fingerprints became visible under the beam of a black light. "We're in luck," he said, taking a close-up picture of the prints. Then, lifting the piece of flagstone, he placed it in the spot where they conjectured it had been removed. The flagstone fit so perfectly, an observer would have been hard-pressed to see that it was hiding something underneath.

"Well, I'll be darned," Jamie gasped. "It looks like we may have found the very briefcase Dad used to pay the ransom. This is unbelievable, Lance. How do you suppose it could have lain there undiscovered all this time?"

"I don't know, Jamie. That one has me baffled, too. Hopefully, the briefcase itself will hold the answer to that secret."

A thought came to Jamie. "Do you suppose the kidnapper might have been reckless enough to leave fingerprints on the briefcase?"

"I'd say there's a good chance of it. The man obviously knew he had outsmarted the law by grabbing the ransom right out from under their noses. He could have hidden the empty briefcase here figuring it would never be found. Criminals do make mistakes."

"So if he did leave prints on the briefcase, could they still be detectable after all this time?"

"There's an excellent chance of that. I once lifted a good set of prints off a picture frame of a man who had been dead more than seventy years. That's while I was still in school. I got an A for that project." Lance turned to look at the open door leading to the room where he and his mother had been held captive. Jamie could sense his anguish as he stood motionless, just staring at it. "Going in there isn't going to be easy," he said at last. "But I need to check it."

Jamie wished there were something she could do to ease his pain. Almost without thinking, she reached out and grasped his hand. She immediately wished she hadn't. Lance glanced at their hands, then lifted his eyes to meet hers. She hoped he wouldn't notice how her heart had sped up. He didn't say a word, nor did he remove his hand. He just turned, and together they started for the door leading to the dreaded room.

CHAPTER 20

Ivan pulled the Buick Century off the rental lot and drove straight for his office. He was glad to see Allison was still with him. "You knew the truth about Lance all along, didn't you?" he suggested.

"Of course I did. I've kept tabs on my grandson from the day he was born. That's one of the advantages of being a guardian angel."

"A guardian angel? Is that what you are, Allison?"

"Have been nearly since the time I entered my present world. I've been assigned to you, Lance, and Jamie—all three. I was assigned to Rene until she crossed the line to join me on this side."

Ivan's smile was especially warm as he considered his wife's words. "Thinking of you as an angel is easy," he remarked dreamily. "I considered you an angel from the first day we met."

Allison returned his smile. "Different meaning of angel, sweetheart. But that's okay by me. I love having you think of me that way." A softness filled Allison's eyes as she thought of her world and how she would like to explain more. "There's so much more I wish I could share with you, Ivan. But, you'll just have to wait—it's the rules."

"Can you at least tell me how I'm supposed to face my grandson after all these years? I'm scared to death, Allison."

"What's to be scared of, sweetheart? Lance is a wonderful young man, and he didn't exactly grow up totally missing out on the man his granddad was. I was there telling him about you nearly every night of his life. With my help, blame and dislike never festered in his mind."

"I'm confused, Allison. You've told me I'm the only one you've been permitted to show yourself to, and now you say you talked with Lance. I don't get it."

"As angels, we're rarely permitted to show ourselves to those we work with as I've been permitted with you. But there are other means of communication between our worlds, Ivan. Take Lance, for example. When I speak to him, he hears me as a gentle, guiding voice from deep within his own heart. I can only reach him if he's willing to listen. With Lance, that's always been the case. His listening to me, I mean. Just as it's always been the case with you, Ivan."

Ivan flipped on his turn signal and moved into the right turn lane as he approached the next stoplight. Pulling to a stop, he waited for the traffic to clear before making the turn. "Are you saying you were here with me even before I was able to see you?" he asked incredulously.

"I think you already know the answer to that, don't you, Ivan?"

Ivan adjusted the glasses a little higher on his face. "Yeah, I guess I do. I think I've known you were with me ever since the day we shared our last good-bye kiss. Truth be told," he laughed, "I was more sure of your nearness that way than after you suddenly showed up for my eyes to see."

"That's natural, sweetheart. I completely understand how you might perceive me as unreal. I suppose that's one of the reasons for the rarity of guardian angels working this way. But, for your information, you're not the first who's been permitted to hear my natural voice. Lance holds that honor. Not that he actually saw me, like you've been allowed to do, but he did hear my voice. It was at the time of the kidnapping, when he was making his escape and became lost in the woods. Lance has always believed it was his mother who guided him to safety, but it was really me."

"You were allowed to talk to Lance? To lead him to safety?" Ivan asked.

Allison nodded. "Rene begged the authorities to let her do it, but they felt she was too emotional for such an early assignment. They reached a compromise and sent me instead. That's the only time Lance heard my natural voice. After that, I became a gentle, guiding voice in his mind."

Ivan pulled forward into the turn. "I find that very interesting," he remarked. "Do we all have guardian angels with us?"

"Yes and no," she attempted to explain. "There are those who refuse to listen to their guardian angel. When this happens, more often than not, the angels assigned to them turn their energy to more constructive matters. There's always much to be done on our side, sweetheart, and time's far too precious to be wasted. In my case, I've had little trouble communicating with those I'm assigned to."

"Meaning Lance, Jamie, and me?" Ivan guessed.

"Precisely."

This brought up another question. "Then, may I assume you knew Jamie even before I adopted her?"

"I've known Jamie all her life, Ivan. I was there keeping an eye on things the day she was born. I was also there that awful day when she watched her biological parents ripped away in a rage of violence."

Allison's explanation of this triggered another question in Ivan's mind. "You know who really murdered Rene, don't you?" he probed.

She sighed. "I know, yes. But I'm forbidden to tell you, if that's what you're hoping for."

Ivan eased down on the brake as the movement of traffic slowed. "How is it you're not permitted to tell me who murdered Rene, but you are permitted to tell me that Lance and Jamie are destined for each other?"

"I don't make the rules, Ivan. Someone with a lot more knowledge than me has that responsibility. I only abide by the rules as they're laid out for me. I was given specific permission to tell you about Lance and Jamie. Otherwise I couldn't have done it." Allison leaned back in her seat and brushed her hair off one shoulder. "You've been asking me a lot of questions, Ivan. Let me turn the tables on you. From our conversation, may I assume you've finally accepted me as real and not just a figment of your imagination?"

Ivan contemplated her question. After a moment, he glanced over at her and their eyes met. "I do believe you're real now," he quietly admitted. "I don't understand how it's possible, but I am convinced that you've been given some sort of special permission to visit me this way."

Allison's eyes lit up. "Hallelujah!" she shouted. "It's about time! So are you glad I've been allowed to come to you like this, or not?"

Ivan grew somber. "You can't know how wonderful it is having you with me like this," he said. "But, be honest. It isn't going to last, is it? You will be leaving me again, won't you?"

"Oh, Ivan, I'm so sorry. Yes, I will be leaving you again when my work at this level has ended. But I'll still be near you, just as before. And we will be together again when your time here is finished."

"When your work on this level has ended?" he repeated. "When will that be?"

"Very soon, sweetheart. Things are coming together according to the celestial plan that brought me on this assignment."

Ivan lowered his eyes. "I was afraid of that. I've lived long enough to know that we're given certain experiences intended to teach us something of value, and I understand these experiences usually don't come cheap. Been there, done that, more times than I can count at the moment." He paused before adding, "Your being here is one of those experiences, isn't it? I'm supposed to learn something, but it's going to cost me, right?"

"It might cause you some short-term pain, sweetheart, but in the end it will set you free."

"Free?" He questioned. "Free from what?"

"The reason I'm here," she explained, "is because you were throwing your life away by wallowing in a pool of guilt. I was allowed to come here to help you learn how to forgive yourself."

"And, say I do learn how to forgive myself?" he proposed. "That's when you walk away again, isn't it?"

Her eyes lowered. "I'll still be here, but we just won't be able to communicate like we're doing now."

"It's going to burn a hole through my heart, losing you again."

"I know. But I also know you'll be a better man for what you've learned, sweetheart. A better man now, and a better man forever."

Ivan felt sick inside. How bittersweet it was now that he had put aside all doubt of Allison's reality. Knowing she was really here with him this way left his heart filled with indescribable joy. But knowing it was to end soon left him to deal with a reality nearly as bitter as losing her to cancer in the first place. Through it all, he knew she was right. He would be a better man for the experience, just as long as he learned the lesson she was there to teach. Like she said, a better man for now, and a better man throughout forever. Beyond doubt, this was one lesson that wouldn't be learned without a steep price.

CHAPTER 21

Lance only released Jamie's hand when they reached the doorway leading into the smaller room, where he paused long enough to check the doorknob for fingerprints. There were some smudges but no clear prints. "I'm a little amazed that this door is still on its hinges," he remarked, pulling it closed to see even the latch still worked. "I assume vandals got to the front door over the years, but for some reason they left this one untouched."

Lance pushed the door open again and, after brushing away the cobwebs, entered the room with Jamie close behind. The dust lay just as thick in there as it had in the first room. As Jamie looked on, Lance moved to the single window. Gripping the three iron bars, he found them all still solidly in place. "Can you believe Mom actually squeezed me out between these bars?" he stated. "I still remember how much it hurt."

Though Jamie didn't respond, she did allow a mental picture to develop in her mind of how it must have been that day. She was sure it must have hurt when Rene forced Lance out through those bars, but she wasn't sure which one it hurt the most. What a horrible thing for a mother to be forced to do—send her little boy into these mountains alone knowing it was his only hope for survival.

She quietly watched as Lance meticulously covered every inch of the room for more clues. She wasn't the least bit surprised when nothing new turned up. They'd already found a lot more in the place than she would have guessed.

At last he paused and just stood looking the room over from corner to corner. "Funny how much bigger it looked through the eyes of a five-year-old," he remarked. One more brief moment just looking, and he stated, "I guess that pretty much wraps it up in here. I would like to take a look around outside before we leave."

Mention of the outside reminded Jamie of something she hadn't recalled until now. "I just remembered something about my dream, Lance!" she exclaimed. "Part of the dream went beyond the day I came here with my dad. For some reason, you were in the dream, and you were checking out that gorge next to the cabin. You found something in the gorge. I couldn't make out what it was, but I do remember how excited you were over finding it. I know this is a crazy idea, but the rest of my dream was on the money. Do you think you should check out the gorge?"

Lance shook his head. "This is a strange experience for me, Jamie," he acknowledged. "I'm trained to deal with hard evidence, not dreams. But I can't deny your dream led us to the exact place of the crime. Let's go check that gorge."

Gathering up his bag of equipment, Lance led the way out of the cabin. Allowing time for their eyes to adjust to the sunlight, he walked to the gorge and stared down into it. "Two hundred feet deep, I'd guess," he said as Jamie joined him. "Maybe two hundred fifty."

"Be careful," Jamie warned, noticing how close he was to the edge. "You're not wearing a *light fall* suit, you know." Jamie realized it was a dumb joke, but it had just slipped out.

"Light fall suit?" Lance laughed. "Good point, but I'd like to get a better look at what's down there, and I can't do it from ten feet back."

Jamie grabbed an arm and held on tightly as he leaned over the edge. If this bothered him, he didn't show it. "Would you look at this?" he said after several seconds of searching the area. "You may have been onto something in your dream, Jamie. There's an object on a ledge about twenty feet down. I can't quite make out what it is, but it's definitely man-made."

Jamie felt her skin prickle as the accuracy of her dream flooded her mind. It was almost frightening. "I have some rope with my things," Lance explained. "I think I'll make a loop and see if I can snag whatever it is."

Lance opened his bag and pulled out a fifty-foot roll of light-weight nylon rope. One end he fashioned into an adjustable loop.

Jamie was glad to see him lie down with only his head and shoulders over the edge this time. This seemed much safer than standing so near the edge, as he had done before. She watched as he lowered the rope and fumbled around with it for what seemed an eternity. "I got it!" he called out at last. "Now if I can just tighten the loop without letting it slip off." Another eternity passed before he exclaimed, "I've got it, Jamie! Hang on while I haul it in!"

Jamie drew a relieved breath as Lance stood holding his trophy for both to see. "What is it?" she asked.

"I'm not sure. It might be some sort of electrical-control device. Whatever it is, it's pretty old. It's made with transistors that were obsolete years ago. But there's a manufacturer's tag. With any kind of luck, I can pull a part number out of the rust."

Lance glanced back at the gorge. "I wonder what else might be down there?" he said. "Do you know anyone who's into rappelling by chance?"

"As a matter of fact, I do," Jamie assured him. "My partner, Milton Taylor, is highly skilled at rappelling. He has all his own gear, too."

Jamie noticed Lance glancing at her left hand. "The engagement ring?" he offhandedly remarked. "Milton's by chance?"

Jamie felt the blood rush to her face. Why should it bother her that Lance noticed Milton's ring? Whatever the reason, she couldn't deny it was bothering her. "Yes," she quietly admitted. "Milton and I haven't actually set the date, but we are engaged."

"I'd say Milton is a lucky man," Lance declared. Then, as if wanting to get away from the subject, he looked around at the surrounding mountains. "My memories of this place aren't good ones," he remarked. "But I bet the memories of you and your father coming here on horseback are better."

"Horseback riding is great fun," Jamie assured him. "You should try it sometime, Lance."

"Any chance you could give me a lesson or two?" he asked, rolling up his rope.

Jamie had to bite her lip to keep from shouting *YES!* But what would Milton think about her giving riding lessons to another man? "We'll see," she forced herself to say. "But for now, what do you say we do our riding in a helicopter? If we're finished here, that is."

CHAPTER 22

Jamie stepped into her apartment, flipped on the light, tossed her purse and keys on the sofa, then headed straight for the refrigerator for a cold drink. She had just put in two grueling days, and she was ready for some relaxation. Lance's offer for dinner had been more tempting than she dared think about. Not that she was all that hungry; there was just something about Lance's company that left her feeling like a schoolgirl hoping to be asked to the prom. But she had turned down his dinner offer guessing that Milton would probably want to spend the evening with her.

She popped the tab on her can of soda and took a sip while trying to shake off such thoughts. The phone rang, and she checked the caller ID to see it was Milton. That was no surprise, since it was now 6:30. Milton was a creature of habit, and one of his habits was calling her just before leaving the office. He always left at precisely 6:30. She felt naughty as thoughts of not answering crossed her mind—not that it would do any good anyway. If she didn't answer the phone, Milton would just call her cell phone. She picked up. "Hi, Milton. How was your day?"

"It was good. I got a ton of work out of the way. What's up with you? I expected you'd be in the office sometime today."

"I'm sorry, Milton, I should have called. It's been one of those days. If you're in the mood to take a hungry lady to dinner, I'll fill you in."

"You read my mind, beautiful. Is half an hour okay?"

"Perfect."

"See you at seven then."

Jamie dropped the phone and mentally scolded herself for wishing she could be having dinner with Lance instead of Milton. What was the matter with her, anyway? Three days ago she didn't even know Lance, and now it was all she could do to keep him from her thoughts. Picking up the phone again, she punched in her father's number only to reach his answering machine. Not bothering with a message, she tried his cell phone. This time he answered. "What's up, Dad?" she asked. "I figured you'd be home by now."

"Yeah, I'm running a little late," he explained. "So, how'd your day go?"

"Better than you can imagine, Dad. The cabin I told you about, well, it turned out to be the right one."

"You're kidding me!" Ivan exclaimed. "Did you discover anything of interest?"

"Did we ever! We may have even found the briefcase you used to deliver the ransom money. Lance took it to his lab to see if it might yield any hidden clues."

"You found a briefcase?" Ivan asked in obvious shock. "What makes you think it could be mine?"

"For one thing, it has your initials on it."

"My initials?" he gasped. "Describe the briefcase to me, Jamie."

"Okay. It was large—much larger than the one you use today. It was black with two latches, one on each end of the case, and a combination lock in the center. Your initials were on an oval-shaped, silver plaque just to the right of the lock."

"That's incredible! A perfect description. And you found the thing in that cabin after all these years?"

"We found something else, too. Some sort of electronic device Lance estimates was from the same era as the kidnapping. He has that at his lab, too."

"Lance sounds like an amazing young man, Jamie. He's certainly done wonders for my cause, with your help, naturally. Thanks to what you two came up with, I think there's a good chance my charges will be thrown out of court. So, have you had supper? I can swing by and pick you up, if you like."

"Milton's picking me up, but you're welcome to join us, Dad."

"No, I'll grab something at the house. Enjoy your evening with Milton."

"Thanks, Dad. Love ya."

"Love you too, baby."

Jamie was glad when she learned Milton had called for reservations at the Outback Steakhouse. She loved the way they seasoned their steaks, but most of all she loved the "Bloomin' Onion" they served as an appetizer. Jamie waited until their order was placed before beginning an explanation of what she'd been up to the past couple of days. She started with the part about her father being set up as a suspect in the Wagner murder case. She was a little surprised that Milton hadn't heard about it on the news, but he had evidently been too busy catching up to take time for television. "Why didn't you call me?" he asked, sounding a little upset. "You know I'd have dropped everything and been there to help."

"I know, Milton, but I figured you needed time to get over your jet lag. We pretty much had everything under control."

"We?" Milton questioned with raised eyebrows. "Meaning you and your new friend, Lance Gentry?"

Jamie unfolded her napkin and nervously smoothed out the crease. She had casually mentioned Lance earlier in their conversation, briefly explaining he was a police officer from Orlando who was there on a special case. Evidently this was enough of a clue for a detective like Milton to piece the rest together. "Lance is a highly skilled forensic crime investigator," she explained. "He was standing next to me when I heard about Dad's dilemma. He offered to help, and—"

"What about Ivan?" Milton broke in. "Is he in custody?"

"He was, but he's out now. Together, Lance and I uncovered enough evidence to practically ensure clearing Dad's name." Jamie was angry at herself for feeling so jittery about this conversation. She had done nothing wrong. The time she and Lance spent together was strictly professional, nothing more. She was glad for the distraction when the server stepped up to the table with their drinks and the "Bloomin' Onion."

"Sounds like the two of you did a good job," Milton said as he stripped his straw and slid it into his drink. "Did you finger the actual killer while clearing your dad's name?"

"We found some pretty strong evidence that points to a Sylvester Jarvis. The problem is, no one knows the whereabouts of Jarvis. He just got out of prison two months ago on parole, and he's vanished."

"Lovely," Milton quipped. "But if your dad's off the hook, that's the main thing for now. So, tell me more about this Lance. What's the special case he's here working on?"

Jamie caught a quick breath. Talking with Milton about Lance wasn't the easiest thing to do, but she knew Milton deserved to know the whole story. She toyed with where to start and eventually asked, "Are you aware my father had another daughter long before I came into his life?"

Milton stiffened. "I'm aware of Rene, yes. But I didn't know you were." He cleared his throat. "Ivan's threatened me with fire and brimstone if I ever let it slip. So, how you did you find out?"

Jamie pulled off an onion strip, dipped it in the sauce, and nibbled at the end of it. "I basically found out about Rene from Lance," she replied, seeing no advantage to bringing up the stranger in the overcoat at the moment. All that could be filled in later. "You see, Milton, Lance is Rene's son."

"Rene's son? That's right, I do remember stories of her having a son."

"You can probably guess that the case I mentioned Lance working on is his own mother's."

"I see," Milton said, rubbing his chin. "Sounds like an intriguing challenge, going back to look at a case that old. I assume you've become involved?"

"Yes." Her answer came with a firmness surprising even herself.

Milton took a drink of soda. "How about your father?" he asked. "Is he aware that you know about Rene?"

A bit of a feisty smile crossed her lips. "He is now," she affirmed.

Milton squirmed for a more comfortable spot in his chair. "I hope you know how badly I feel about keeping these things from you," he apologized.

Jamie reached across and patted his hand. "I understand," she calmly stated. "My dad can be pretty convincing when he wants to be."

"That he can," Milton agreed with a sigh. "Thanks for understanding."

Jamie glanced up to see the hostess just stepping up to their table. "Is your name Milton Taylor?" she asked.

"I'm Milton, yes," he answered.

"There's a telephone call for you, sir. You can take it in the bar section."

Jamie and Milton exchanged glances. "That's odd," he observed. "Why would anyone call me here? Did they identify themselves?" he asked the hostess.

"No," she said. "They just described a Mr. Milton Taylor who was here with a young woman and asked if I would call him to the phone. I thought you two fit the description."

Milton pushed back his chair and stood. "Excuse me, Jamie," he said. "I'll see what this is about and be right back."

The hostess hesitated as Milton left the table, then, as he rounded the corner at the end of the aisle, she spoke to Jamie again. "I know you're going to think this strange," she said. "But I'm just the messenger. The person on the phone asked me to pass along a message to you as soon as the gentleman you're with went to answer the call."

"What message?" Jamie asked as one eyebrow arched.

"I'm supposed to tell you your father is in the parking lot in his Lexus. He wants to see you right away. He asked that I tell you without your gentleman friend hearing."

Jamie was confused. Why would her dad do something like this? She could only conclude it had something to do with the Wagner murder. Maybe some new complications had arisen. Only one way to find out. "Thank you," she said as she stood and headed for the door.

Once in the parking lot, Jamie had little trouble spotting her dad's Lexus. Her heart raced as she noticed he was parked in the darkest corner. Why would he do that? Hurriedly, she crossed the lot to his car.

CHAPTER 23

Success in a forensic lab was nothing new to Lance, but thanks to the elements of nature combining to preserve two quarter-century-old pieces of evidence, the abundance of success from this evening's effort astounded even him. There was the briefcase, which he had little trouble pinning down as the probable one Ivan used to pay the ransom, and the electronic device found in the gorge outside the cabin.

The briefcase proved to be covered with fingerprints, some quite old and some fairly fresh. Extracting identifiable samples from the older prints was more difficult, but with painstaking effort Lance did pull up a few that were useable. These, he discovered, were made by two separate individuals, one of whom he positively identified as his grandfather, Ivan Barker. This pretty much eliminated all doubt that the briefcase was authentic.

The second set of older prints he couldn't identify right away, but he did discover something very interesting about them. They were made by the same person as the fresher prints on the briefcase. This was an unexpected twist in the investigation. Lance had assumed some passerby must have accidentally found the briefcase while rummaging around in the old cabin. But since these prints matched, it pointed to a different theory. Whoever had handled the briefcase twenty-five years ago had also handled it again just recently. It could reasonably be assumed the original prints were made by the kidnapper, and if this were the case—it could also be assumed the kidnapper was still alive. Not only was he alive, he had returned to the crime scene for some reason. This left Lance with more questions than answers.

The electronic device was another matter. It was too weatherworn to provide any fingerprints, but it did yield something of grave importance. The name tag was made of brass, which wasn't affected by rust. It took some work, but Lance was able to extract enough information to know the gadget was manufactured by Radio Shack. He was even able to pull up the manufacturer's part number. One of Lance's good friends from Orlando, Ralph Burger, was an executive in the company. Once Lance had pieced the information together, he placed a long-distance call to Ralph hoping to learn more about the device. Half an hour later, Ralph returned Lance's call with the good news. Radio Shack still had records of the old device in their archives. It turned out to be a transmitter, and from what Ralph explained, Lance was able to piece together the answer to a mystery that had eluded everyone for twenty-five years. He knew now how the kidnapper had gotten the ransom money from the trash can completely undetected.

Lance desperately wanted to share the good news with Jamie. He toyed with the idea of calling her but thought better of it when he remembered how anxious she had been to get home by 6:30 in case Milton should call. Reason told him she was probably out with Milton now. "That Milton Taylor is one lucky man," Lance heard himself say. He had to laugh at himself for it. Truth be known, if Milton wasn't in the picture, Jamie would find Lance's shadow on her doorstep pretty darn fast. The funny thing was, Lance didn't even know why he found her so attractive. He wasn't much for socializing, and he dated only occasionally. But there was something about Jamie, something he couldn't put a finger on, that made him feel as though he'd been looking for her all his life. "Knock it off!" he grumbled to himself. "This is all nonsense. Jamie's engaged to Milton Taylor, end of story."

If he couldn't share the news with Jamie, the second-best thing would be sharing it with Uncle Charley. This brought a grin to his face, thinking how excited Charley would be when he discovered how the money was taken from that trash can right under his and Sheriff Quinn's noses. Lance picked up the phone and punched in the number for Charley's cell phone. To his disappointment, the call rolled over to Charley's answering service. He concluded Charley either had his phone turned off or was someplace where he had no service.

"It's me, Uncle Charley," Lance said, leaving his message on the recorder. "I have some news I'm dying to share with you. Call me ASAP. I'm at the lab. I plan on being here most of the night."

Lance hung up his phone and turned his attention back to the DNA samples he'd been running tests on. There was the sample taken from beneath his mother's fingernails at the time of her murder, the sample taken from the blood on the handkerchief belonging to the man he strongly suspected had killed Samuel Wagner, and a sample of saliva he had extracted from under the stamp on the letter his anonymous benefactor had sent to Charley, bringing the two of them here to reopen his mother's case.

The first sample he pulled up on his computer screen was from the anonymous donor. Something about this DNA pattern immediately caught his eye. There were striking similarities in this pattern to his own DNA signature. Was it possible? . . .

When he left Orlando he had brought along a few items he thought might prove useful in researching his mother's murder. One of those items was a CD containing some personal data, including a sample of his own DNA, as well as a sample of Uncle Charley's. Retrieving the CD, he inserted it in the computer and promptly pulled up samples of his and Charley's DNA, which he displayed alongside the pattern already on the screen. "Would you look at this!" he exclaimed excitedly. "The odds are off the scale that the benefactor is a relative of mine!" Lance studied Charley's DNA. "He's no match for Uncle Charley, that's for sure," he remarked. "That would mean if he is my blood relative, he's someone from my father's side. But who?"

Lance knew his father had been abandoned as an infant and grew up in an orphanage. He never even knew who his parents were. Lance also knew now that the anonymous donor was a man, since Jamie saw and talked with him. "Is it possible I've just discovered two grandfathers in my life?" he questioned. "Or, maybe an uncle on my father's side who might have learned about my situation?"

Lance had no way of knowing it, of course, but he wasn't alone in the lab at the moment. Allison had popped in on him a short time back, just to see what progress he was making on Rene's case. "Well, now," she remarked. "You've been a busy little beaver, haven't you, Lance? Listen to what I'm telling you, sweetie. What you're looking at on that computer screen is interesting, but it's not what you should be spending your time on. You're here to solve Rene's murder. I can help you do that if you'll just let me."

"This is all very interesting," Lance sighed. "And it's something I definitely want to check further into, but right now I need to be checking other things." He cleared the screen and brought up a new image on it. This time it was the DNA pattern from the bits of flesh taken from Rene's fingernails.

This brought a huge smile to Allison's face. "You are listening to me!" she exclaimed. "Okay, let's get down to work. I want you to think of this: you're not investigating just one crime, you're actually investigating two. You're looking for evidence in Rene's murder, and you're looking for evidence to clear your grandfather's name in Samuel Wagner's murder. Think outside of the box, Lance. You have evidence at your fingertips that can blow these cases wide open."

Lance leaned a little closer to the screen. It was an awesome and completely eerie feeling knowing he was looking at the DNA signature of the man who killed his mother. There had to be some way to attach a name to this sample. That was his biggest challenge at the moment—finding a way to attach a name to it. The evidence indicated the killer was still alive, and if that were the case, Lance couldn't rest until the madman was brought to justice. "What am I overlooking here?" he mulled. "I have the strongest feeling something is staring me right in the face, but what?"

"Samuel Wagner," Allison said, her lips only inches from Lance's ear. "Think Samuel Wagner."

"Why do thoughts of Samuel Wagner's murder keep coming to mind?" Lance asked himself. "I'm looking at my mother's murderer here." He pulled a copy of a fingerprint taken from the briefcase to the computer screen and displayed it alongside the DNA pattern. Now he sat staring at two pieces of evidence containing the still-hidden identity of his mother's murderer. Yet, thoughts of Samuel Wagner refused to leave his mind. On an impulse, he divided the computer screen into two halves, leaving the evidence he already had up on the left section. On the right section, he pulled up a copy of a fingerprint he had extracted from the bloody handkerchief.

"Now you're cooking," Allison pressed. "Look closely, Lance! What do you see?"

"Wait a minute!" Lance suddenly cried, staring at the fingerprint on the left section of the screen, then at the one on the right section. "Is it possible?" He moved one print over the other and gasped at what he saw. Instantly he brought the DNA sample from the blood on the handkerchief to the screen and overlaid it with the DNA taken from under his mother's nails. "They match!" he shouted. "Sylvester Jarvis murdered my mother!"

"You're doing fine, Lance," Allison said more confidently now. "Just reason it out one step at a time."

"It all makes sense. Jarvis got the money from the trash can, where Granddad placed it. He then came back to the cabin, where he discovered I had escaped."

"Yes!" Allison affirmed, realizing Lance was understanding her. "Jarvis panicked because he was afraid you might lead the authorities back to the cabin. In his haste to cover the mistake, he hid the brief-case, money and all, under the flagstone slab, which he had prepared ahead of time for just such an emergency. He couldn't chance leaving Rene's body anywhere near the cabin, as that would lead to a search that might uncover the money. He forced her in his car and drove several miles away to a spot just off Highway 260, where he killed her and dumped her body in a dry gulch. It was his intention to recover the money after a month or so, when the heat was off. But as he was trying to flee the area, he was caught in a high-speed chase and taken into custody. That's when it was discovered he was wanted on an outstanding warrant for the murder of Arnold Pointer, the man he had killed in a barroom brawl."

"That's it!!" Lance exclaimed excitedly. "Granddad sent Jarvis to prison, where he remained until two months ago when he was paroled. That's just about the time the briefcase was taken from its hiding place in the cabin."

Lance considered the irony of what his grandfather had done. He had sent Rene's killer to prison without even realizing it. "No wonder Jarvis hates him so bitterly," Lance surmised. "But I have enough evidence to put him away for good this time."

Suddenly another terrifying thought crossed Lance's mind. If Jarvis had done his homework, he would know that Ivan had another daughter now. Was it possible the man's hatred for Ivan wouldn't be satisfied with simply framing him for murder? Was history on the verge of repeating itself? Lance grabbed the phone and punched in Jamie's number. This was one time he didn't care if Milton might be the jealous sort—Jamie had to be warned.

CHAPTER 24

Ivan grabbed a towel and stepped from the shower. The warmth of the plush, white throw rug felt good beneath his bare feet. The shower had felt good too, after a very long and very trying day. He finished toweling himself off, then slipped into a robe when the phone rang. "That'll be Jamie," he told himself, hurrying to the family room, where he kept a cordless phone. A glance at the caller ID told him otherwise. It was a call from Milton Taylor's cell phone. Why would Milton be calling at this hour? "Hello?"

"Ivan," Milton said, a hint of concern showing in his voice. "Is everything okay? Is Jamie with you?"

"What?" Ivan countered. "What do you mean is everything okay? And why would you think Jamie is with me?"

There was a pause before Milton asked, "Were you at the Outback Steakhouse tonight?"

"Milton! You're not making any sense! Slow down and tell me what this is all about. Does it concern Jamie?"

"Yes!" Milton nervously responded. "Jamie and I were dining at the Outback Steakhouse on Clearview Avenue when I was called to the phone. The caller was a man who sounded intoxicated. I couldn't make sense of what he was saying. When I finally got something out of him, I learned he'd been paid twenty bucks to make the call and keep me on the line as long as possible. I rushed back to the table to find Jamie gone. According to the hostess, she had stepped outside to meet you, Ivan. You were supposedly in the parking lot in your car."

"What!" Ivan bellowed. "Something is terribly wrong, Milton. I don't have my Lexus—it came up missing at the police compound. Did you check the lot for Jamie?"

"Of course I checked the lot, but by the time I got there, there was no sign of her or your car."

Ivan felt an icy ripple of fear penetrate his spine. He had no idea what was going on with this, but it obviously wasn't good. His jumbled thoughts were disrupted by the sound of someone at the door. "Come on in!" he called out. "It's open!"

"What?" Milton asked.

"Someone's at the door, Milton," Ivan responded as Sheriff Quinn burst into the room with Charley Stapleton right behind him.

Quinn came straight to Ivan and, pointing a finger at the phone, he mouthed the words *Your phone is bugged! Hang it up!* From the expression on Quinn's face, Ivan knew instantly this was no joke.

"Milton, just hold your tongue and listen!" Ivan promptly instructed. "Stay at the restaurant! Do not leave the restaurant, do you understand me? Rene would want it that way!" Ivan threw the part about Rene in to key Milton in that something was wrong. Apparently it worked, as Milton didn't bother to reply, but simply hung up.

Ivan dropped his phone back on the hook and would have said something if Quinn hadn't placed a hand over his mouth. Quinn then grabbed a Post-it note and pencil from the table next to the phone and scribbled a fast note. *Your whole house may be bugged. Throw on some clothes and we'll talk in my squad car.*

By this time a cold sweat had broken out on Ivan's brow as he knew whatever was happening had something to do with Jamie. He rushed to the bedroom and threw on some clothes. None of the men spoke until they were in Quinn's squad car and pulling away from the house. "What's going on?!" Ivan pressed. "What do you mean my house is bugged?"

"I don't know that for sure, Ivan," Quinn admitted. "But I'm not taking any chances in light of what's happened. Show him the letter you found on your door, Charley." Quinn flipped on a map light over Ivan's seat.

"You're not going to like this, Ivan," Charley said, handing Ivan the letter. "It's happening again, just like twenty-five years ago. I found this letter not half an hour ago. I called the sheriff right away, and he picked me up. We headed straight for your place."

With shaky hands, Ivan unfolded the page and began reading

aloud. *Hello, Ivan. It's been a long time, hasn't it? But I'm sure you will remember me.*

"Oh, no, not again!" Ivan gasped in disbelief as he continued reading.

We're going to do this much the same as we did before. You'll find another trash can exactly where the last one was. This one, too, is marked with yellow ribbon. I want the drop made at exactly two o'clock tomorrow morning. Only this time, I'm upping the ante to $2 million. You shouldn't have any trouble raising the money, especially since you're out on bail. It might be a little harder for you if you were locked up in that cold cell. Oh, yes, I do know about your problem, Barker. I know you killed some poor soul and will soon be standing trial for murder.

Ivan looked up again. "The kidnapper knows about Samuel Wagner?" he asked in a trembling voice "I don't get it."

"Neither do I," Quinn admitted. "But it's obvious he knows. Read the rest of it."

Ivan moved the letter back under the light. *Shame on you, Barker. Now you'll have to rot out the remainder of your days in a stinking cell. That breaks my heart. As for your daughter, we both know you have very little chance of ever seeing her again. But unless you do exactly as I say—your chances will be zero. I'm not dumb enough to think you'll keep the law out of this. You brought them in on it before, for all the good it did you. That's okay, it adds a little excitement to the game. All you have to do is catch me when I go after the money, and you might save the girl's life. But remember, Barker, I outsmarted you once, and I'm betting I can do it again. No tricks. Just come alone, and so help me, if anyone approaches the trash can before dawn, they'll be blown into too many pieces to count. Nice doing business with you, Barker. Think of me often, and when you do, picture me basking on some exotic beach nestled up to a bottle of the finest wine your money can buy. It's your move. You will pardon me if I don't wish you luck?*

"Hang in there, Ivan," Quinn said as Ivan raised his eyes to stare through the windshield into the darkness of the night. "We're going to get this guy this time."

"He abducted her from the Outback Steakhouse on Clearview Avenue, where she was having dinner with Milton," Ivan hastily stated. "That was Milton on the phone when you came in. Whoever the kidnapper is, he evidently has my Lexus. He sent a message to

Jamie that I was in my Lexus in the parking lot and that I wanted to see her alone."

Quinn grabbed his radio mike and called for the police dispatcher to get on the line. "This is Brenda, Chief," came an instant reply. "What do you need?"

"I need an APB out on a stolen car. The man driving it is extremely dangerous and probably armed." Quinn handed the mike to Ivan. "Give her a description of your car," he barked.

Ivan keyed the mike. "It's a five-month-old, dark green Lexus LS430. License number ZLD 707."

Quinn grabbed the mike back. "Did you get that Brenda?"

"Got it, Chief. I'll get right on it."

"While you're at it, send someone to the Outback Steakhouse on Clearview Avenue to pick up Milton Taylor. We're on our way to headquarters now. I want Milton there ASAP. I need to ask him some questions."

* * *

After allowing Jamie's phone to ring several times, a message came on telling Lance the cell phone he was trying to reach was not in service at the time. What should he do? He knew Jamie could be in grave danger. On an impulse, he tried Charley's number again. This time he got through, and after only one ring. "Lance!" Charley shouted, having obviously checked his caller ID. "Where are you, kid?"

"I'm at the lab, Charley, and have I got news for you! But first things first—I think Jamie may be in grave danger!"

Lance wasn't prepared for what Charley told him next. "Jamie's been kidnapped," he barked. "I found a ransom note on my motel door just like I did on my apartment door twenty-five years ago. It's the same guy, kid. This is unbelievable!"

"Oh, no!" Lance gasped. Then, gathering his wits, he hastily shouted out his own news. "I know who has her, Charley! And I know where he's probably taken her."

"You know what?" Charley spit back. "Wait a minute! Let me turn the volume up on this phone so we all can hear. I'm with Ivan and Sheriff Quinn."

"Good! Good! Can you all hear me?!"

"We hear you!" Quinn replied. "What is it you want to tell us, son?"

"I know who has Jamie!" Lance repeated. "And I know where he's probably taken her!"

"What are you saying?" Quinn loudly questioned. "What do you know? And how?"

"It's Sylvester Jarvis!" Lance exclaimed. "The same man who killed Samuel Wagner. I have the proof!"

"Sylvester Jarvis?!" Quinn bellowed. "You're positive?"

"Completely positive! The man's out to get Granddad, just as we assumed. You say there was a ransom note? Does he want the money delivered the same way as before?"

Lance heard Ivan gasp in the background and remark, "He called me Granddad." Lance had slipped in saying it, but at the moment he didn't care.

"According to the ransom note, the guy wants everything done the same as before," Quinn explained. "Do you have a reason for wanting to know that?"

"I have a big reason!" Lance affirmed. "I know how he got the money out of the trash can without you seeing him! And I know how to foil his plan this time!"

"Where are you, son? I'll send someone to bring you to police headquarters, where we can talk."

* * *

By the time Lance arrived at headquarters to join the others already there, including Milton, Ivan's stomach was churning, and his mind was in a daze. How could this be happening again? Lance took a seat at the conference table, where the others were already seated. "All right, son," Sheriff Quinn told him. "You've got the floor. Fill us in on what you know."

For the next ten to fifteen minutes, Ivan and the others listened to Lance's explanation of what he and Jamie had discovered at the old cabin, what facts he had later uncovered at the lab, and most interesting of all—how Sylvester Jarvis had gotten the money out of the trash can the first time around. The whole thing sounded so surreal. Ivan glanced up to see Allison enter the room, and his heart leapt with hope. He had no idea where she had been since disappearing from his car as he was driving home earlier in the evening, but he was ever so glad to see her now.

"I'm not allowed to tell you everything I know," she said, smiling. "But just have faith in our grandson. He knows what he's doing. I've been helping him all evening. I've been with Jamie, too. She's all right for now, and if everyone does their job, she'll be back in your arms very soon." Ivan felt a wave of relief. If Allison said Jamie was okay, then that left him without the slightest doubt to the contrary. "Just remember one thing," Allison added. "From here on out, you're going to have to share Jamie's arms with someone else, and I think you know who I mean." Ivan let his eyes move to Milton, then to Lance, and finally back to Allison. He nodded "yes." And happily so.

"I have a plan worked out," Lance explained. "But we'll need two helicopters. Can you arrange for these, Sheriff?"

"We have one in the department as you know, son. I'm sure I can borrow another chopper and pilot from Luke Air Force Base. The base commander is a good friend of mine."

"I want you to know it's important that a helicopter be borrowed from Luke Air Force Base," Allison explained to Ivan. "For your information, we guardian angels often work quite closely with each other. I just had Sheriff Quinn's angel put the idea in his head. Neat, huh?"

CHAPTER 25

A bright stream of moonlight played against Jamie's face. Even though her eyes were open, everything around her appeared to be in a dense fog. Where was she? How did she get here? Why couldn't she remember? As her mind began to clear a little, she realized the moonlight was filtering through a small window at the end of the room. What was it about this room that seemed so familiar? Why did its four gray walls send such a cold chill through her very soul? In the midst of her confusion, she thought she heard a voice calling her name.

She tried to answer, but only coughed as a pungent odor filled her nostrils. What was the odor? It was something she associated with hospitals. Chloroform! That was it—but she knew she wasn't in a hospital. Then, from somewhere deep in the chambers of her mind, a picture started to form. She was walking toward her father's car. Something was wrong, he had said, and he wanted to talk with her. For some reason he had parked in the darkest section of the lot. She could barely see him through the dark tint of his window.

She covered her mouth in horror as the memory continued. When she reached the car, the door flew open and something was pressed tightly against her nose and mouth. She drew a petrified breath as the sharp tang of chloroform penetrated deep into her lungs. For a time, she struggled to free herself, but as the black walls of unconsciousness closed in on her mind, her struggling became more and more labored.

Again, she fought to clear her mind. How long ago had that been, and who was calling her name now? Little by little her eyes began to focus until she discovered she was looking into a very lovely set of eyes. They seemed darker and more penetrating than any eyes she had ever seen. "Jamie," the soothing voice called again. "Are you awake?"

Jamie looked more closely at the woman now. She was radiantly beautiful, with raven black hair and was in a stunning white dress that seemed to glow in the dim light of the room. "I—I think so," Jamie groaned, struggling to sit up. "My head won't stop spinning. Oh—and my stomach. What's happened to me? Where am I?"

"Something very unpleasant has happened, Jamie," the beautiful woman explained. "I think, once your head sufficiently clears, you'll recognize where you are."

A rush of panic gripped Jamie as she realized she did recognize the place. Laboriously, she made her way to her feet, then stood on wobbly legs, trying to sort things out. She had obviously been abducted and brought to this room, the same room she and Lance had visited only hours before. But who was this woman with her? Had she been abducted, too? "Who are you?" Jamie asked. "And how did we end up in this place?"

"This is a bit complicated, I'm afraid," the woman explained. "My name is Rene. I've been given permission to be here with you in your hour of trial."

"Rene?" Jamie gasped, struggling to understand. "Are you saying you're Rene Barker?"

Rene smiled. "I was once a Barker. Actually, I'm Rene Gentry now. You should know that. You've heard my story."

"Oh my!" Jamie struggled. "If you're that Rene, then I must be . . ."

Rene shook her head. "No, little sister, you're not dead. I'm an angel and, as I said, I have permission to be here with you. You see, Jamie, I know exactly what you're going through, and I couldn't bear to let you go through it alone."

"You couldn't?" Jamie asked, wrestling to clear the remaining cobwebs from her mind.

"No, I couldn't. Let me explain something, Jamie. You don't know me, but I know you quite well. Though I've remained unseen, that doesn't mean I haven't followed every step of your life, little sister."

Jamie was amazed at the bond she instantly felt with Rene. Rene didn't feel like a stranger at all. "You called me 'little sister'," Jamie observed. "Do you really think of me as your sister?"

"You are my sister, Jamie. No one was happier than me when our father made you part of the family."

Under different circumstances, Jamie would have wanted to pursue this part of the conversation further, but looking around she realized what dire straits she was in. "I've obviously been kidnapped," she remarked. "And I've been brought to the same cabin a kidnapper brought you to twenty-five years ago." Jamie hesitated a moment, then guessed, "It's the same man, isn't it? He's come back after all these years to take me away from Dad, just as he once took you away."

"That's right, Jamie. And when you learn who he is, it may come as a shock."

"You can tell me who he is?" Jamie asked in surprise. "Angels are allowed to do that?"

"Only when we're cleared by those in authority. The man's name is Sylvester Jarvis."

"Sylvester Jarvis?" Jamie gasped. "The man who's trying to frame Dad for Samuel Wagner's murder is the same man who—who? . . ."

"It's okay to say it. Sylvester is the man who murdered me. And he's the same man who kidnapped you. He's doing this for two reasons. The first one is greed. He wants more money from our father. His second reason is revenge. He hates our father and wants to exile him to a cold prison cell for the remainder of his life."

"That's not going to happen, Rene!" Jamie exclaimed. "I'm sure being an angel, you must know the evidence Lance and I uncovered proving Dad's innocence."

"I know," Rene answered smiling warmly. "But Sylvester Jarvis doesn't know. Because of that, your life is in great danger."

Jamie took a deep breath. "Then, I am going to die? Is that what you're telling me?"

Rene's smile faded. "I wish I could give you a definite answer, Jamie. But the truth is, I'm not even permitted to know the answer myself. I do know there's an excellent chance you're going to make it through this alive. Lance knows several things that give the police a big advantage this time. He knows you've been kidnapped, and he knows Sylvester is the one who did it. He also knows how Sylvester successfully retrieved the ransom in my case. And he knows about this cabin. All these things are heavily in your favor, Jamie."

Jamie brushed a hand through her hair. "Then there is a good chance Lance might save me?"

"A very good chance, little sister. I know something else about Lance that'll be of great interest to you too. And I have permission to share it."

"You want to tell me Lance and I could have a great life together, is that it?"

Rene laughed. "Looks like your guardian angel has been whispering a few things in your ear, little sister."

"I've known from the moment I first saw Lance, but I just wouldn't admit it. Is that little voice in my head that won't leave me alone my guardian angel, by chance?"

Rene's smile deepened. "It is."

"But what if Sylvester Jarvis *does* kill me? Won't that cancel out anything Lance and I might have had together?"

"Doesn't work that way, Jamie. If you and Lance fail to find each other here, you'll find one who will make you happy. That's not to say you will or won't make it through this, but it is to say everything will work out."

Jamie retreated into thought a moment or two. "I knew there was something about Lance when I first met him," Jamie admitted. "And maybe I shouldn't ask this, but the thought has crossed my mind. If Lance and I should marry, will you and I still be sisters? Or? . . ."

"Or will I be your mother-in-law?" Rene laughed. "Don't let it confuse you, Jamie. Those in authority will work it all out. Just remember, we'll always be sisters regardless of what other titles are tacked on." Rene grew more solemn. "I want you to know I understand the depth of your love for our father. I know I made some mistakes when I was in this world, the greatest of which was not telling him how much I loved him. I caused him a lot of grief for many years. That's something I'm pretty ashamed of. But I want you to know I love him just as much as you do."

"Then—you're saying you've forgiven him for what he did to you and Neil?"

"Yes, Jamie. Neil and I will be together forever, and forever is a very long time. I know Neil has forgiven him, too."

Jamie glanced around at the gloomy room that held her prisoner. "I hope you know how grateful I am to have you here with me," she told Rene. "When you went through it, it must have been terrible."

"It was the hardest thing I ever went through in my life," Rene admitted. "Right up to the time Lance escaped. I thought my heart was going to break as I watched those little legs take him down the road and out of my sight. After that, a wonderful thing happened. I had an angel come to stay with me."

"An angel was here with you?" Jamie asked.

"Yes. Right here in this room. In my case, it was my mother. She remained with me all the way to the end. Then, she escorted me home. It was a beautiful experience."

"Dying is a beautiful experience?" Jamie remarked. "That's hard for me to grasp."

"It's hard for any mortal to grasp until they go through it for themselves."

"That's such a beautiful story, Rene. There's only one thing I would have thought might have been different. I would have thought that Neil would have been the one to 'take you home,' as you put it."

"Neil was busy with other pressing matters at the time," Rene explained. "Otherwise, he would have been the one. Are you frightened?" she asked, changing the subject.

"Yes," Jamie answered with an attempted laugh that didn't quite make it. "But the truth is, I'm more worried about what it might do to Dad if he loses a second daughter this way. He's not a young man anymore, Rene. I have no idea what might happen to him."

"Dad will be all right no matter what," Rene comforted. "He's a strong man, Jamie. I know that's of little comfort to you now, but when you find yourself on my side of forever, you will understand. No matter what, Dad will be okay."

"Does he know yet?" Jamie asked.

"He knows. And I can tell you something else that might make you feel better. Mom is with him now, just as I'm with you."

Jamie closed her eyes as tears trickled down her cheeks. "Allison is with Dad?" she asked. "He can see her and talk with her like I'm doing with you?"

"Yes, little sister. Isn't that wonderful?"

"More than wonderful," Jamie sniffed, unable to hold back a new flood of tears. "Thank you, big sister—for everything!"

CHAPTER 26

In the early morning darkness, Charley huddled behind a fallen log with Ed Quinn on his left and Milton Taylor on his right. Gripped with a feeling of déjà vu, he remembered another night he and Quinn had spent on this very hill, overlooking this same campsite, and feeling this same determination to stop a venomous snake before it had the chance to strike. There was a moon tonight, a nearly full one. Maybe that was a good omen. The night twenty-five years ago had been moonless. "We're going to nail this guy this time," Sheriff Quinn whispered, never taking his night goggles off the campsite below them.

"And we're going to bring Jamie home in one piece," Milton quickly added.

Charley only wished he could feel that certain. Granted, they were much more prepared this time thanks to everything Lance had uncovered. But this Jarvis was a shrewd one, and he had proven more elusive than a jungle cat on the prowl. He had a way of covering all his tracks, like avoiding Sheriff Quinn's APB on Ivan's Lexus. The car was abandoned less than two blocks from the restaurant. Jarvis obviously had another set of wheels stashed there for a quick exchange.

Without question, Lance's plan was well laid out, but it did have one flaw. It depended on Jarvis sticking close to his original pattern and not tossing in any unexpected changes along the way. According to Lance's theory, Jarvis was a man who would stick to a pattern that had proven itself in the past. As for Charley, he just wasn't sure.

"There's Ivan now," Quinn suddenly stated. "He's about to make the drop."

Charley lifted his night goggles to look for himself. It was Ivan, all right. "Everyone in place," Charley quietly whispered. "It's show time."

* * *

Ivan's stomach churned as he left the car and hurriedly moved to the marked trash can. Everything was exactly as it had been twenty-five years ago. A cold chill gripped him at the thought this could be happening again. But this time he knew the madman's name. And this time, he wasn't alone. "She's going to be all right," Allison whispered in his ear. "Just have faith, my dearest husband."

"Are you sure of that?" Ivan asked anxiously.

"Look at all Jamie has going for her," Allison argued. "Jarvis doesn't have the upper hand this time like he did with Rene. It will work out differently this time, Ivan. I may not know that as an angel, but I do know it as a mother."

Ivan stopped just short of the trash can and glanced around for evidence that what Lance had told him was real. Jarvis had done a good job hiding his handiwork, but with Ivan knowing what to look for, and aided by the light of a full moon, he was able to confirm it. He pulled the briefcase to his chest and stared at the open can. "Do you know what terrible memories this is stirring for me, Allison?" he asked.

"I know," she comforted. "And I know what a tragedy losing Rene was to you, but just think of it this way. Adversity always brings opportunity for growth. Out of that tragedy has come a lot of good."

"What good?" Ivan countered.

"For one thing, you're a much stronger man because of it, Ivan. Look at the kind of father you've been for Jamie, and how you turned her life around. And that's only a fraction of the good that came from it."

Ivan wished with all his heart he could more fully understand and believe what Allison was saying. But how could he? She was an angel with a broader perspective than his. He was still a mere mortal. He made a vow to work harder at understanding the message Allison was so diligently trying to convey to him.

Taking the final step up to the trash can, he stared down into it. Squinting his eyes to help penetrate the darkness, he could barely make out the shape of something else Lance had theorized would be there. His courage further bolstered, he dropped the briefcase inside and hurried back to his car.

"So tell me, Allison," he remarked as he put the car in gear and pulled out onto the road. "Have you known from the beginning that Jarvis was the one who murdered Rene, and that I sent him to prison on another charge?"

"Yes, Ivan, I've known. As an angel I was allowed to watch the ugly episode unfold. I hope you'll understand I was forbidden to tell you."

"And now, you're forbidden to tell me if Jamie will be okay?"

"The difference is, in Jamie's case I don't know the outcome myself. The authorities have guarded that part very closely."

"Tell me again, Allison, why am I allowed to see and talk with you the way I'm doing now? I mean, it's obvious your authorities have strong rules about what can and can't be done. Why have they approved you to be here like this?"

Allison sighed. "I went to the authorities on your behalf, Ivan. I know what a stubborn man you can be, and I know how hard it is for you to forgive yourself for past mistakes. But if you don't forgive yourself, it will bring some eternal consequences to our family. I convinced the authorities that you needed a little extra help, and they approved my visit. It's something they don't easily approve of."

"It was your idea?"

"Yes."

"Well, I'm glad you did it. It's been wonderful."

"But?" she pressed. "Has it been successful? Have I convinced you to forgive yourself?"

Ivan didn't hesitate with his answer—he had already come to grips with this one. "Yes, Allison," he admitted. "You have been successful. I'm not there yet, but I'm on the way to forgiving myself. It'll take a lot of work, but I won't let you down. You have my word on it."

Her smile grew warmer. "Then my work here is nearly finished," she said.

Somehow Ivan knew this would be the result of his confession. Thoughts of Allison leaving again tore at his heart, but at least now he had a restored hope for being with her again in a new dimension that would stretch forward into the halls of forever. He would be with her, with Rene, with Neil, and hopefully somewhere many years from now they would be joined by Jamie and Lance. He had to smile thinking that if Jamie and Lance had children, and their children had children, the forever family could continue to grow in ways he could only begin to understand now. A thought was forming in his mind that this thing of forever was worth any cost that could be paid. Even the cost of losing the presence of one he loved so dearly here in this world—to the hideous crime of murder.

* * *

Charley watched Ivan's car disappear down the moonlit road, apparently on its way back to town just as it had with Rene. But Charley knew the plan was different this time. "Okay, the drop's been made," Sheriff Quinn said. "That's our cue. Let's go."

The three men made their way up the mountain to a small plateau where the police helicopter waited. The plan was to pick Ivan up at the base of the mountain, then to keep track of the radio transmitter Ivan had hidden in the briefcase. Charley hoped Jarvis wasn't wary enough to check the case over before moving on with his plan. Lance had assured Charley he wouldn't, and so far, Lance had been right about everything else.

Actually, the tracking device was only a backup addition to the original plan. If all went according to schedule, they knew where Jarvis was headed. The tracking device would only be needed if he went someplace other than the old mountain cabin.

* * *

Roughly an hour had passed since Jamie had awakened to find an angel with her when the familiar sound of a helicopter reached her ears. "What is that?" she asked. "Is it coming here?"

"You'll find out in a very few minutes, Jamie," Rene smiled. "As for me, it's my cue to be running along."

"You're leaving me?" Jamie anxiously asked.

"I was only authorized for one brief visit, little sister."

Jamie felt somewhat frightened at the thought of being left alone. And she felt an ache in her heart knowing this choice time with a newfound sister was about to end. "I want a favor from you," Rene asked, leaving Jamie wondering what sort of favor an angel could ask of her. "Just in case you get the chance, tell Dad I said I love him, okay?"

"I will," Jamie responded, brushing away the tears. "If I'm allowed to see him again myself, that is."

While Jamie watched in awe, this beautiful angel gradually became enclosed in a blanket of light that seemed to fold around her like fingers from a giant hand. The last thing Jamie saw was Rene's smile, and then the room became dark and cold. Moving to the window, Jamie watched as the helicopter eased to the ground right in front of the cabin. Strong landing lights illuminated the area with great intensity. A man jumped out, and her heart skipped a beat as she recognized Lance. She saw he was carrying a pistol. He rushed inside the cabin, and seconds later she heard him yell through the locked door. "Are you in there, Jamie?"

"Yes!" she shouted back over the sobbing that now racked her body.

"Stand clear of the door! I'm going to shoot the lock off!"

"I'm clear!" she shouted back. "Shoot the blasted thing and get me out of here!"

There was one loud report followed by another a second or so later. Then came the sound of him fumbling with the latch—and the door flew open, leaving her staring into the most welcome face she had ever seen. On an impulse she rushed to him and threw herself into his arms, where she stood shaking with emotion. She wanted to feel his arms around her, but he only held her lightly at the shoulders. What could she expect since she was wearing another man's ring? "Are you all right?" Lance asked. "Did he hurt you?"

Reluctantly, Jamie pulled back a step, still staring into those incredible eyes. "He used chloroform on me," she choked. "Other than that, I'm okay—I think."

"Come on," Lance said. "Let's get you out of here." Taking her by the arm, he led her hurriedly outside, where she drew in a welcomed breath of fresh air. "Get in the chopper," he said. "We have to set out the welcome mat for our kidnapper."

Jamie hesitated before climbing inside. "Why not call him by name?" she suggested. "We both know he's Sylvester Jarvis."

Lance looked surprised. "You figured that out?" he asked. "Way to go, Jamie!"

Jamie smiled through glistening tears, which refused to stop flowing. Lance didn't need to know she learned about Jarvis from an angel. What harm would it do for him to think she figured it out on her own? "Well, it was pretty obvious," she said. "Once you looked at all the facts."

"Yeah," he agreed with a grin. "I guess that's right. Now get in the chopper. We have work to do."

Jamie could see the chopper more clearly now. It was a small, two-person military craft. She could just make out the image of the pilot, who remained at the controls. Lance opened the door and handed the borrowed pistol back to the pilot, then moved aside so Jamie could climb in. She snapped her seat belt as he slammed the door, then felt a lurch as the chopper shot abruptly upward. "Is Lance going to be okay here by himself?" she asked the pilot.

"We aren't leaving him alone, Jamie," came a stout, male voice that Jamie was almost sure she had heard before. "I'm going to touch down over there behind that clump of heavy brush where the chopper will be out of sight. We'll stay here as Lance's backup until more help arrives."

Jamie strained to see the pilot's face, but there just wasn't enough light. It took only a couple of minutes for him to move the chopper. Once it was down again, he cut the engine and shut off the lights. "We'll be unnoticed here," he explained. "But we're in a position where we can see what's going on at the cabin."

Jamie strained even harder to see the man. Why couldn't she place where she had heard his voice? She was just about to ask if they had met when her attention was drawn back to the road leading up to the cabin, where a set of headlights suddenly knifed through the darkness. It had to be Jarvis returning. Her heart raced, thinking how close she had come to still being in that cabin.

CHAPTER 27

It was less than half an hour before sunup when Sylvester Jarvis pulled his Ford Ranger to a stop in front of the old log cabin. He grinned, thinking to himself how the explosion at the rigged trash can must have rocked the air only minutes earlier. Once again, the evidence of how his brilliant plan was accomplished had vanished in a puff of smoke. It was just like old times, only better. This time, there would be no brat kid to mess things up. All he had to do now was kill the girl, dump her body in the gorge, then drive away to the new life he had mapped out for himself in the Canary Islands—a life he would have started enjoying twenty-five years ago if it hadn't been for that meddling old fool, Ivan Barker. It was a long time in coming, but Barker was about to pay for his interference. Jarvis touched the briefcase on the seat next to him and mused at how sweet life was about to become. There hadn't been time to open the briefcase yet, but he was certain the $2 million was in it. Ivan Barker would cough up ten times that amount if he had the slightest hope it would spare his daughter's life.

An evil laugh erupted from Jarvis's lips as he savored the moment. Things may have gone terribly wrong the first time he played out this scenario with Ivan Barker, but this time he was home free. Not only did he have the $2 million, he still had the $500,000 he had not been able to enjoy the first time. It was knowing the $500,000 was waiting for him that made all those years in that stinking prison cell bearable. That, and his plan to hit Barker where it hurt again. Fortunately, Jarvis had enough contacts on the outside to keep close tabs on Barker all those years. He probably knew more about Barker than

Barker knew about himself. And now it was Barker's turn to face the prospect of waking up every morning surrounded by four cold walls. He probably wouldn't even be allowed to attend his daughter's funeral.

Placing a thumb on the briefcase latch, Jarvis gave it a push. It didn't budge. He tried again only to realize it was locked. "What is this, some kind of joke?" he spit out. "That old fool can't possibly think a little thing like a lock will keep me from my money."

Jarvis opened the door and stepped out of the Ranger, then placed the briefcase on the ground. Pulling a large revolver from beneath his coat, he took aim at the latch and was about to squeeze off a shot when the sound of a man's voice caught his attention. "I wouldn't do that if I were you, Jarvis!"

Lurching back to the Ranger, Jarvis crouched next to it and scanned the moonlit area for signs of who had spoken. As his mind settled, he realized the voice had come from the briefcase itself. Puzzled by this strange turn of events, he jumped when the voice came a second time. "Make any attempt to open this briefcase and your whole world goes up in a flash of fire and smoke! This may come as a shock to you, Jarvis, but you're not the only one with a trick up his sleeve!"

Jarvis's mind spun in confusion as he groped to sort this out. The voice definitely came from the briefcase, but was it a recording or was he being watched from some remote location? Again, he looked around nervously, but spotted no one. He tried to remain calm. Reason told him the voice had to be a recording, since he had covered every inch of his tracks, including being absolutely certain he wasn't followed. Unless? . . . Was it possible his Ranger had been spotted at Roosevelt Lake, where he had picked up the money? It was highly unlikely—but he had to admit—it was possible. That could mean he had unwittingly transported a stowaway here to the cabin. It could also explain how a perpetrator knew his name. He could have gotten it off the registration papers in the glove box.

Tightening the grip on his gun, Jarvis rose for a look inside the Ranger. No sign of anyone there. It would have been virtually impossible for anyone to have climbed out of the Ranger without Jarvis seeing him. The voice from the briefcase had to be a recording—it was the only logical explanation. Of course, that left the unanswered question of how they knew his name.

Jarvis inched his way back to the briefcase and stood looking down at it. The voice had hinted it contained a bomb. Jarvis rolled his eyes at the preposterous thought. He knew Ivan Barker wouldn't do anything that foolish when his daughter's life was at stake. Then it hit him. He hadn't delivered the ransom note directly to Ivan. He had delivered it to that stupid brother-in-law, Charley Stapleton. Delivering a ransom note to Charley Stapleton was easier than risking exposing himself trying to deliver it to a famous lawyer. His chances of getting caught were much less that way. This was Jarvis's same line of reasoning when he used Charley as a go-between the first time around.

Maybe he had made a big mistake. Maybe the bad blood between Ivan and Charley went deeper than Jarvis had assumed. Maybe Charley went straight to the police and never even told Ivan. Jarvis shook his head. That couldn't be right. He had been watching when the money was dropped, and if it wasn't Ivan who dropped it—it was his twin. None of this made any sense.

Jarvis stared at the briefcase and weighed his options. He could kill the girl and take the briefcase someplace where he could set up a temporary workshop. That way, with his knowledge of explosives, he could easily disarm any triggering device that might be present. But this plan contained one huge flaw. What if the money really wasn't in the briefcase? With the girl dead, he'd lose his leverage for ever getting the $2 million. No, he had to know now if the money was inside. Kneeling down, he drew a hand across the case, feeling for any hint of a triggering device. There was nothing obvious.

As he considered his next option, a movement in the shadows at the edge of the cabin caught his eye. Leaping to his feet, he stared disbelievingly at the silhouette of a man who had appeared from behind the cabin and was walking toward him. His first inclination was to believe the earlier assumption—there had been a stowaway in his Ranger. Jarvis raised his gun and pointed it straight at the man's heart. "Hold it right there!" he shouted, knowing full well he couldn't squeeze off a shot—in the light of the moon, Jarvis could see the man was holding what appeared to be a remote detonator. If the briefcase did contain a bomb, it meant this man had already armed it, and it was set to go off if he released his grip on the detonator. If Jarvis were to kill the man, he would relax his grip on the detonator and Jarvis would be killed by the bomb. All Jarvis could do was look on in horror as the man walked to within fifteen feet of him and stopped.

"I'm sure you know what this is," Lance said, holding up the detonator. "And just so you'll know, there's enough explosives in that briefcase to vaporize you. The way I see it, you have only one choice and that's to do exactly what I say."

Jarvis's head pounded and every inch of his body retched with bitter contempt. How had he gotten himself into this mess? He moved his gun until it pointed directly at the detonator. He knew he was a good enough shot to take it out. What he didn't know was whether or not a bullet would disable the device before it could trigger the explosives. He was wise enough to realize the chances of this weren't in his favor.

"I want you to slowly turn around," Lance instructed. "Once you're facing that gorge behind you, I want you to throw your gun into it. Do you understand what I'm saying, Jarvis?"

Jarvis swore under his breath. "Who are you?" he growled. "How do you know my name?"

"All in good time, Jarvis. Right now, get rid of the gun."

For a long moment, Jarvis stood frozen. When he spoke, it was to offer a proposition. "Listen, what do you say we make a deal, okay?"

"No deals, Jarvis! Turn around and get rid of the gun."

Jarvis glanced anxiously around again to see if he could spot anyone else. It appeared this guy was working alone. That was good. Jarvis had little doubt he could take the guy if he didn't have any backup. Insofar as the gun was concerned, getting rid of it was of little consequence since he had a backup plan of his own.

Jarvis had no idea if this guy was a cop or an opportunist who saw the chance to make a few bucks. One way or the other, Jarvis figured money talked pretty loud. Maybe this guy would take the bait if the right offer were dangled in front of him. Not that Jarvis would actually honor any deal to split the money, but he might use it to grab the upper hand. "All right, pal," he gruffly relented. "I'll lose the gun. Just don't do anything stupid."

Slowly, Jarvis turned around. He estimated the gorge was about fifteen feet away. It would be no trick at all, tossing the gun into it. But why not play it smart? If he judged his throw just right, the gun would land at the edge of the gorge, where it could be retrieved in case of an emergency. Taking careful aim, he swung his arm and let the weapon fly. Just as he hoped, it landed only inches short. Turning back to face the man, he shrugged. "I guess I misjudged the distance." Then, drawing a nervous breath, he made his move. "Look, I'm willing to consider a deal here, if it's money you're interested in. The stakes are high, you know. Two million." The words rolled temptingly off his tongue. "Half that in your own pocket would go a long way toward making life very pleasant. Know what I'm saying, pal?"

"Is that what you think?" Lance asked. "That I'm interested in part of your blood money?"

Jarvis let out a burst of gruff laughter. "What? Are you going to play righteous on me? Think about it, pal. A million bucks. You'd be set for life."

Lance shook his head in disgust. "And just how long would my life expectancy be dealing with a liar like you?" he asked. Not waiting for an answer, he added, "I noticed a couple of things about you, Jarvis. One, you're left-handed. And two, you have a bandage on your right arm."

Jarvis glared at the man. "So I'm left-handed, so what?" he blurted out in contempt. "And, it's none of your business, but the bandage is for a scratch I got working on my car."

"I don't think so, Jarvis. I think you took a bullet in your right arm as you fired the fatal shot that killed Samuel Wagner. It was a left-handed man who killed him, you know. Which definitely rules out Ivan Barker."

This revelation hit Jarvis with a jolt. The guy knew about Wagner, and he had Jarvis pegged for the killer. Was this guy a cop or not? If he was a cop, it meant the plan to send Barker to prison had back-fired. "I don't know no Samuel Wagner!" Jarvis lied as his mind raced for answers.

"Oh, you knew Samuel Wagner, all right. You're the one who set Samuel up for murder in the first place, knowing full well he'd hire Ivan to defend him. Then you could put the rest of your plan in motion by killing Wagner and pinning it on Ivan. Too bad you were too stupid to pull it off, Jarvis. You are a stupid man, you know."

Anger ran through Jarvis's veins like floods of molten lava. How dare this young fool accuse him of being stupid! "Who are you?" Jarvis demanded with rancor.

Lance smiled. "Who am I? I'm your biggest nightmare, Jarvis. Ever hear the name Lance Gentry?"

Jarvis's eyes narrowed as he considered the name. For some reason, it did strike him as being familiar, but he couldn't place exactly where he'd heard it. "Should it mean something?" he growled.

Lance deliberately shuffled the detonator back and forth between his thumb and fingers, catching Jarvis's attention. "I'm a little surprised my name doesn't ring a bell, Jarvis," he said tauntingly. "Maybe we need to jog your memory. Let's start with this cabin, what do you say? You have seen this cabin before, haven't you?"

Jarvis's attention was riveted on Lance as he tried to figure out where he was going with this. His immediate response came only as a hardened stare. "The truth is, you've been here on more than one occasion," Lance continued. "The last time was about two months ago. That's when you recovered the money you'd hidden here twenty-five years ago when you kidnapped and killed another young woman. Is your memory getting any better yet?"

Great beads of sweat formed on Jarvis's brow. "You don't know what you're talking about!" he snarled.

"Oh, but I do," Lance assured him. "I'm talking about the $500,000 you extorted from Ivan Barker. You know, the money you had him drop in the trash can at Roosevelt Lake."

Jarvis bit his lip and shifted his weight nervously. "You're out of your mind!" he spit out. "I don't know nothing about no ransom money!"

Lance simply ignored his denial and stated emphatically, "I know how you did it, Jarvis. You dug a narrow trench from the lake to the spot where the trash can was located. You flooded the trench with water and covered it with plywood and dirt so it wouldn't be noticed."

Jarvis ground his teeth as he listened in disbelief to an exact account of how he had recovered the money. Who was this young punk, and how had he figured this out?

"You removed the bottom from the trash can," Lance went on. "You positioned the explosives beneath it and rigged them to go off, using a timer set for the hour of dawn. Am I getting close?"

Jarvis stared with contempt at this meddling fool who obviously had everything figured out.

"Okay," Lance said. "Let's put the finishing touches on your scheme. You positioned a rather large remote-control boat under the trash can. You bought the boat from Radio Shack, by the way."

"Lies!" Jarvis desperately spit out again. "All lies!"

"When Ivan Barker dropped his briefcase into the trash can, it fell through the false bottom into your remote-control boat. You positioned yourself on the opposite side of the lake, where you could use night-vision goggles to monitor the pickup point. Once Ivan made the drop, it was a simple matter for you to navigate the boat through the homemade channel and onto the open lake. Once it was on the lake, you simply guided it home. You made sure the explosives were powerful enough to erase all evidence of your complex scheme." A wry smile crossed Lance's face. "You know what I'm betting, Jarvis? I'm betting if I look in the back of that Ford Ranger, I'll find another remote-control boat. Still want to claim ignorance? Even with your hand glued inside the cookie jar? Oh, and just for your information, Jarvis, we had a bomb squad on the scene to disarm your explosives this time. We'll have all the evidence at the Roosevelt Lake pickup site intact for your next trial date."

"Who are you?" Jarvis demanded again. "And what is it you want?!"

"Well, to start with," Lance responded. "I'm someone a lot smarter than you. And what I want is to see you brought to justice for killing my mother."

"Your mother?" Jarvis spit back venomously. "That's where I've heard your name! You were the five-year-old brat that got away!"

"What do you know," Lance grinned. "Your memory is improving."

"No!" Jarvis shrieked. "You cheated me out of what was rightfully mine once! I should have killed you when I had the chance!" Jarvis continued staring at Lance as he formulated his next move. *This young fool thinks he's smarter than Sylvester Jarvis, does he? Well, we'll see just how smart he is when he gets a look at my backup plan.*

CHAPTER 28

The pilot had been right—he and Jamie did have an excellent view of the moonlight meeting between Lance and Sylvester Jarvis. She was delighted to learn she could hear the conversation between the two men, thanks to Lance's expertise. Lance was wearing a hidden microphone which transmitted every word to a small radio receiver in the chopper. Lance could also turn on a speaker in the briefcase, which is how he caught Jarvis's attention in the first place.

Lance seemed to be in charge of the situation at the moment. Nevertheless, Jamie was very concerned. She knew Jarvis was a cold-blooded killer who was extremely devious. Jamie glanced over at the pilot, who was still enough in the shadows to reveal nothing more than a silhouette. "Are the two of you acting alone?" she asked. "Or is there more help on the way?"

"There's another chopper headed this way even as we speak, Jamie," the pilot replied. "Sheriff Quinn's aboard, along with your dad, Charley Stapleton, and Milton Taylor. And, I assume, Sheriff Quinn has an army of officers on their way in squad cars."

Suddenly something clicked in Jamie's mind. She recognized the pilot's voice. "You're the one who spoke to me in the Fry's parking lot!" she exclaimed. "You're a helicopter pilot? This is all very confusing!"

"I wondered how long it would take you to recognize me," the man calmly replied. "I'm sure you have a million questions, and you'll soon have even more." He paused a moment before adding, "It's time I introduced myself. This may come as a shock. You see, Jamie, I'm Neil Gentry."

"Neil Gentry?" Jamie gasped. "But, I thought? . . ."

"It's all right, Jamie. The entire world thinks I'm dead. That's the way I want it. You're one of only two people who know. I think you'll understand better when I tell you my whole story. It all started on January 27, 1973, the day my chopper was shot down in Vietnam. Bart Madoc was the pilot, and he and I were the only two on board. I was thrown free from the chopper and knocked unconscious. The next thing I remember is waking up a couple of weeks later in a hospital back in the States. I'm not sure how it happened, but when the rescue team picked up Bart and me, they got our dog tags mixed up. Bart didn't make it, but by the time I realized what was going on, his body had already been shipped home in the belief it was mine."

"But how could that happen? Surely your families would have realized something was wrong!"

"You see, Jamie, Bart and I had something in common that contributed to the error. We were both orphans, raised without families. Bart's body was mutilated beyond recognition, and DNA testing was far from what it is today. I could have set the record straight, but I didn't. I knew Rene would accept me in spite of what I looked like, but I felt she deserved better than being married to a cripple with no face. I didn't know about Lance, or I might have done things differently."

"So you became Bart Madoc," Jamie quietly remarked. "And let Neil Gentry stay dead?"

Neil laughed softly. "You can't believe how easy it was, Jamie. There must have been a thousand ways to trip me up, but no one ever checked. They just took my word for everything. I was even able to remain in the Air Force. They stuck me behind a desk, naturally, but I found by making friends in the right circles, I could work wonders at breaking the rules. I probably logged more hours flying a chopper off the record than most pilots do legitimately. That's what I'm doing here now, in fact. I was in a meeting with the base commander when Sheriff Quinn called to request a military chopper. I talked my way into being the pilot. I know it's illegal, but old friendships go beyond legal at times. I think you can see that it might cause some people undue problems if the truth ever got out. These are all friends of mine. I want them protected."

Jamie reached out and gently touched Neil's face, causing him to turn and look at her. Even in the darkness, she could make out the eyes of a tormented man. "I'm not saying what you did was right," she tried to comfort him. "But you can't blame yourself for Rene's death. You couldn't have prevented it even if you had been there, Neil."

Neil very gently removed Jamie's hand. "I guess we'll never know that for sure, will we?" he surmised. "By the time I learned of Rene's death, Lance was fifteen years old. Charley had already picked up the pieces and was raising my son for me. That's when I decided to help Lance from behind the scenes. From that point on, I was there watching my son from the sidelines. When I discovered his burning desire to someday solve the mystery of his mother's murder, I resolved to help him achieve that goal. I saw to it he got the right education, and later I set him up with the lab here in Phoenix."

Neil drew in a deep breath. "There's one thing I want you to know, Jamie. I have forgiven myself for my mistakes. After seeing the way Lance turned out, I have to admit that my mistakes didn't hurt him much."

Jamie wiped away a tear. "I'm glad to hear you say that, Neil. Rene's death wasn't your fault, and the rest of what you did is easy to understand. I'm sure you realize now it was a mistake, but I can see why you did it."

"Thanks, Jamie. That means a lot. And as for my investments in Lance, well it looks like they're about to pay off doesn't it? The man who murdered his mother—my wife—is at last about to be held accountable."

Jamie looked back at the scene where Lance and Jarvis were still facing off. "So, how did you learn about me?" she asked. "Did you keep tabs on Ivan too?"

"Yeah, I did. Something else you should know, Jamie. I forgave Ivan for anything he may have done to me a long time ago. I wish I could tell him that, but it would require me being resurrected from the dead."

"I wish you could tell him too." Jamie smiled. "For both your sakes."

Again, Neil changed the subject. "I had no idea things would move this quickly when I decided to get the ball rolling for Lance to reopen his mother's old case. It's a darn good thing I didn't wait any longer. If I'd waited even one more day . . ."

"If you'd waited one more day, I might be the one facing Sylvester Jarvis right now with no one having the slightest idea where to find me."

Neil closed his eyes and turned his face upward. "Sometimes I feel like Rene is here with me. In fact, I felt she was prompting me to hurry and lease the lab and get Lance started on the case."

Jamie toyed with the idea of telling Neil she had seen Rene, but before she could speak, Neil hit her with another bit of shocking news. "I'll be joining Rene in the very near future, Jamie. You see, I'm suffering from an advanced case of melanoma."

"You're dying?" Jamie asked, stunned by the thought.

"Don't shed any tears for me, Jamie. I've been permitted to live long enough to see my son grow into a fine man. And now, I'm about to see Rene's murderer brought to justice. What more could I ask?" Neil hesitated a moment, then went on to say, "I mentioned telling my story to only one other," Neil continued, softening the veil of uneasiness that had accompanied the announcement he was dying. "Are you the least bit curious who the other one is?"

"Yes, very curious."

"I told my son. I explained everything to him on our flight here to the cabin."

"You told Lance?" she asked eagerly. "How did he? . . ."

"He took it quite well, actually. The two of us shared one heck of a cry for two hardened men. He wants the chance to get to know me." Neil paused to wet his lips. "One thing I didn't tell him, Jamie. I didn't tell him I'm dying. Other than my doctor, you're the only one who knows that part."

Jamie brushed a hand past her eye. "Then the two of you are going to have to hurry and make up for all the lost time, aren't you?"

"Whatever catching up we do will have to be fast, Jamie. The doctor gives me about a year to live."

"I'm so sorry," Jamie sobbed. "So very sorry."

"Hey," he said, pulling out a handkerchief and reaching across to wipe her face. "No tears for me, remember."

"I'll try," she sniffed.

"And you will keep your promise, right? The stone at the head of my grave will read *Bart Madoc*."

"You have my word," she quietly affirmed.

"Good." He smiled. "The world will be better for having my little secret buried in our two separate graves. The real Bart Madoc's and mine."

Jamie didn't agree, but she would keep her promise.

CHAPTER 29

The sound of the chopper blades pounded in Charley's ears as he watched the mountainous terrain slip rapidly by below them. He could only hope that Lance's theory had been right about Jamie being held captive in the old log cabin, and that he had arrived in time to rescue her before Jarvis made it back. The chopper pilot knew the exact location of the cabin since she had flown Lance and Jamie up there only yesterday. According to her, the tracking device that had been hidden in the briefcase was directing them to the exact place. Charley glanced over at Sheriff Quinn on the seat just to his left. "How much farther to the cabin?" he asked.

"I'm not sure myself," Quinn declared. "Hey, Pat!" he yelled to the pilot. "How much farther?"

"I estimate another eight to ten minutes, Sheriff," she yelled back. "I'm pushing this bird as hard as I can. If you'll allow me to break radio silence, I can check with the military chopper pilot to learn how things are going."

"No, Pat. Jarvis is a pretty smart cookie, and I don't want to chance that he has a radio tuned to the police frequency. Just keep following the tracking device. We'll know what's going on as soon as we get there."

Pat? Charley thought to himself. *I knew a Pat twenty years ago, and rumor has it she's a chopper pilot now. I wonder? . . . Is this just a coincidence, or could it possibly be? . . .* Charley couldn't see her face from where he was sitting, but his curiosity was just too compelling. He unbuckled his seat belt and moved forward to the seat next to Pat. Looking over at her, he still couldn't be sure. If he was right, the years had been good to her. She was still a knockout. She glanced back at him with a curious look. "Buckle up if you're going to sit there," she barked.

Charley hurriedly obliged. "The sheriff called you Pat," he said.

"That's right, I'm Pat," she affirmed.

"I knew a Pat once," Charley explained. "She was an actress at the time."

Pat's eyes nearly bulged from their sockets as she turned for a better look at Charley's face. "Charley Stapleton?" she gasped in surprise. "It *is* you, isn't it?"

With all doubt dissipated, Charley suddenly wasn't so sure he'd done anything more than open a can of worms. The stories about her becoming a chopper pilot were definitely true, but what about Ted Wolf? Had she and Ted married? Charley's mouth was so dry it made speaking difficult. "Yeah, I'm Charley Stapleton," he managed to say.

The expression on Pat's face changed from surprise to something else Charley couldn't quite read. He wished he could crawl under the seat and make her forget he had ever spoken up. "How have you been, Charley?" she asked after a moment. "Long time no see."

Charley felt as if his heart would explode. Maybe talking to her was okay after all. She at least remembered him, and that was something. He often wondered if she remembered him, and maybe even thought about him now and then. "It has been awhile, hasn't it?" he responded over a very large lump in his throat. "You're looking good, kid."

"I'm looking good?" she bounced back. "After all these years, you suddenly show up in my helicopter, and all you can say is I'm looking good? You're a bigger jerk than I even imagined, Charley Stapleton!"

This wasn't turning into a good experience at all. Charley had been prepared for the possibility that she may have forgotten him. But this? . . . This he wasn't prepared for at all. "I'm a jerk?" he asked, shocked. "What brought that on?"

She sniffed and brushed away what looked like a tear. "What brought that on? Well it might have something to do with an actor who made me fall in love with him, then just walked out of my life without so much as the hint of a good-bye."

Charley scrambled to make sense of what Pat was saying. She fell in love with him? "But, what about Ted Wolf?" he groped. "If you cared anything for me, why were you seeing him?"

"What are you talking about?" she fumed. "Are you out of your mind?"

Charley was sure now that she was crying. Were they tears of anger or something else? "Well? . . ." he stammered. "I did see you and Ted together the night we finished our last performance of *Cats*. The two of you were obviously more than just friends, so I assumed . . ."

"Charley!" Pat tearfully shouted. "Ted Wolf is my cousin!"

Charley's face grew suddenly hot. "Your cousin?"

"Yes—my cousin!" She turned to see his reaction. "Is that why you pulled the final curtain on our act, because you thought Ted and I had something going?!"

"Well—yeah—that's why . . ."

Pat silently returned her full attention to flying the chopper. Charley took this to mean she was finished with this conversation. *Ted Wolf was her cousin?* he mused to himself. *Oh, brother! I really was a jerk for walking out on her.*

He felt suddenly very small. Unbuckling his belt, he eased back to his seat between Ed Quinn and Milton Taylor. Milton leaned over and whispered in his ear. "That woman cares for you, Charley. It sounds like you let her go once, don't be fool enough to make that mistake again."

"Do you really think so?" Charley whispered back.

"I'm sure of it," Milton smiled. "I only wish I could be so lucky with a certain young lady I know. But something tells me we'll never be more than good friends."

"You mean Jamie?"

"Yeah."

"But isn't she wearing your ring?"

"My ring's on her finger, but I'm beginning to doubt I'm the one in her heart. I think that young man you raised is about to ace me out."

"Lance and Jamie? You think so?"

"I'm almost positive of it. I think I've always known in my heart the two of us would never make it to the checkered flag. But that's okay. If we're not right for each other, it's better we find out now than after making vows we might later regret." Milton feigned a smile. "I think I know where Jamie's heart is, and who knows, maybe someday I'll meet the real Miss Right for Milton Taylor."

Charley might have responded, but he was interrupted by Pat's declaration. "There! Just beyond that rise up ahead! That's where the cabin lies."

CHAPTER 30

The sun was just breaking over the eastern hill, allowing Lance a better look at Jarvis's face. Staring into the eyes of the man who deprived him of his mother filled Lance with a flood of emotion. Raw instinct dictated he rip the man's heart out with his bare hands, but cool reason told him that would never do, as it would only drag him down to Jarvis's level. Justice had to be served, but how? What amount of justice could ever balance the scales for what this man had done? As far back as Lance could remember, Charley had told him of his mother's greatest wish. She wished for Lance to grow into a man who loved God, who strived with all his heart, might, mind, and soul to be like the greatest one ever to walk the paths of this earth. What would his mother want him to do if she were here to whisper the answer in his ear now? There was no question what she'd tell him—*Leave temporary justice to the capable hands of Sheriff Quinn and Grandfather Barker.* Then, he knew she would add, *Jarvis's final justice will come from a higher judge, one that Jarvis can never hide from.*

"Answer me one question," Jarvis spoke, pulling Lance from his thoughts. "How do you expect to handle me and at the same time save the girl I have locked up in that cabin? That's a pretty big challenge for one man acting alone, wouldn't you say? Especially when you're up against someone like Sylvester Jarvis."

This struck Lance as odd. How was it Jarvis didn't know he had already rescued Jamie from the cabin, and why would the man think he was acting alone? Then it hit him. Jarvis must have assumed he had gotten here by hiding away in the Ranger. Jarvis had no idea there were others involved.

"We can still do this the easy way," Jarvis spoke up again. "What's past is past. You should be looking to the future, boy. Think of what you could do with a million bucks."

"Put a lid on it, Jarvis," Lance coolly rebutted. "There are some things you don't seem to understand. For one, there is no two million dollars. Ever heard the old adage, 'fool me once, shame on you, fool me twice—shame on me'? Giving you the money didn't keep my mother alive. What makes you think Granddad would believe giving in to your demands now would matter with Jamie? Are you really that big of a fool?"

Jarvis glanced disbelievingly down at the briefcase only inches from his feet. "No money!" he spit back. "You're lying!"

"I'm not lying, Jarvis. There's not so much as one George Washington in that briefcase." Lance stopped short of telling Jarvis there were no explosives there either. So far the bluff had worked nicely, and Lance didn't want to lose that advantage just yet. He knew help was not far away, but there was still some amount of time to continue his stall.

Jarvis's eyes narrowed as he looked up at Lance, then over at the cabin, then back at the briefcase. From the look on Jarvis's face, Lance reasoned the man was up to something. What happened next proved him right. With lightning speed, Jarvis slammed a foot into the brief-case, sending it flying in the direction of the cabin. It came to rest just outside the barred window where Jarvis believed Jamie was still a prisoner. "Go ahead, you young fool!" he barked. "Set off your explosion! But just remember when you do, the girl dies!"

Whirling around, Jarvis made a break for the gun lying at the edge of the gorge. Lance was left with no option other than to try to cut him off. Tossing the fake detonator aside, he burst forward in pursuit of the man. Having the age advantage and the additional benefit of being a trained and physically prepared police officer, Lance caught Jarvis in a flying tackle only inches short of the gun. Instantly, the man pulled a large knife from his boot and pressed a lever, trig-gering the release of a razor-sharp blade. He lunged the knife toward Lance's throat. Lance grabbed the hand holding the knife, and the two men fought for control. Just when it seemed Lance was gaining the edge, Jarvis grabbed a nearby rock with his other hand and swung it toward Lance's head. Lance quickly released his grip and rolled away, causing the rock to miss the mark. Jarvis leaped forward, ending up atop Lance with the knife blade only inches from his throat and the rock posed for another strike. Lance grabbed one of Jarvis's wrists with each of his hands and the struggle was on again.

"Hold it right there!" came the sound of a forceful female voice that caught both men by surprise. Lance glanced up to see Jamie holding Jarvis's own gun only inches from his head. "Drop the knife and the rock!" she shouted. "Or I'll blow what few brains you have all over this mountain!"

A combination of fear and rage burned in Jarvis's eyes as he stared long and hard down the business end of the gun barrel. Very slowly, he released his grip on the knife followed by the rock. Shoving him aside, Lance jumped to his feet. Picking up the knife, he gave it a toss into the gorge. Then, turning to Jamie, he barked, "What are you doing? I told you to stay put!"

"Stay put?" she boomeranged. "You wanted me to stay put when you obviously needed my help? Yeah, right!"

"I could have handled this guy! It's what I'm trained to do!"

"It didn't look to me like you were handling him all that well. I thought you'd be glad to see me."

This discussion might not have ended so abruptly if it weren't for Jarvis jumping into the middle of it. "How did you get out of the cabin?" he snapped, scrambling to his feet. "This whole thing is turning into a real fiasco!" Ripping open his coat, Jarvis pulled out what appeared to be an explosive device of his own. "You see this?" Jarvis shouted. "When I throw this switch, it starts a timer that can't be shut off. After that, fifteen seconds is all you get. I have enough explosive here to blow half this mountain away. Now, give me that gun!"

Lance gave careful consideration to this new development. He realized if the explosive was as powerful as Jarvis claimed, fifteen seconds wouldn't give much time for Jamie and him to reach safety. But neither would it give Jarvis time. The way Lance saw it, they were in the middle of a standoff.

"Now who's holding all the power?" Jarvis pressed on with his bluff. "Things have reversed, only mine's not a fake. Give me that gun!"

"There's more to this scenario than you're admitting," Lance cut in. "We're standing a little close for you to use the bomb without killing yourself in the act. If it explodes, we all die. Or you can set it down and back away from it. That way, we all live. What's it going to be, Jarvis?"

Jarvis nervously wiped the salty sweat from his eyes as it trickled down from his soaked brow to sting like pools of fire. He glanced nervously around, as if thinking he might make a dash for it, thus putting enough distance between them to make using the bomb feasible. "Don't even think it," Jamie warned, tightening her finger on the gun's trigger. "You won't make so much as one step."

"What's it going to be?" Lance asked again. "Do we live, or do we die?"

"It was you who figured it out, wasn't it?" Jarvis tensely accused, staring at Lance. "You remembered the cabin from the time I brought you and your mother here! How could I have overlooked the possibility of you coming back to haunt me? I should have killed you all those years ago when I had the chance. I still would have had your mother as insurance for my ransom demands."

"Set the bomb down," Lance proposed again. "It's over, Jarvis."

"No! I won't go back to that rat-infested cell! I'd rather die right here and now. I'm giving you and the girl one chance to live. Let me get in that Ranger and drive away. That's all I ask. I won't use the bomb, you have my word."

"Your word?" Lance laughed. "I'd come closer to believing a cobra's promise not to strike. And I know something else, too. You're not the kind to choose dying over any other choice looking you in the face. You're a coward, Jarvis. And all cowards are afraid to die. I'm going to walk over there and take that bomb out of your hand. If you do anything to try to stop me, Jamie will put a bullet through your heart. Are we on the same frequency here? Do you understand me, Jarvis?"

Before Lance could take that first step toward the man, the sound of a chopper struck his ears. He turned fully expecting to see the police chopper making an approach, but what he actually saw was the small military craft piloted by the man he had just discovered to be his father. The chopper was fully visible now, as daylight had completely broken. Lance watched it lift from behind the brush and move at breakneck speed toward them. Lance knew his father had been listening to every word of the conversation and was certain of his intention. He was going to place his chopper between them and Jarvis, using it as a shield from flying shrapnel if the grenade exploded. His father was putting his own life on the line to save Lance and Jamie. A glance back at Jarvis found the man totally stunned by what was happening. He was staring at the approaching chopper through terrified eyes and remained frozen in place like a bronze statue.

Lance sprang into instant action. Grabbing Jamie around the waist, he used his weight to force them both as far as possible away from the spot where they'd been standing. When they struck the ground, he gripped her tightly and continued to roll, gaining even more distance. Once he felt they were safe, he glanced up to see the chopper dropping down just in front of Jarvis. It reached a point about a foot from the ground, and there it hovered. Through the open doors, Lance could see a paralyzed Jarvis in a state of confused disarray. He had thought Lance was acting alone, and now he knew that was a mistake in judgement. "No, Dad!" Lance cried as Neil turned to look at him. "Don't do it!"

There were tears in Neil's eyes. He yelled to be heard over the noise of the chopper blades. "I love you, son. I wasn't there for you the first time, but I'm here for you now."

Lance watched in terror as Jarvis suddenly tossed the bomb into the chopper and moved backward as far as he could without falling into the gorge. "NO!" Lance cried again. "You cheated me out of a mother! Now you're taking my father, too!"

Neil had spotted the bomb, but there was little he could do, as there wasn't time to land the chopper and get clear of it. He glanced at Lance one final time, giving him a smile and a wave. Then, gripping the controls, he turned to face Jarvis. In one sideways swoop, the chopper caught the unsuspecting man full on, hurling him over the edge of the gorge. There was a blood-curdling scream as man and machine plummeted out of sight. The scream was cut short seconds later by the sound of a horrendous explosion.

"Dad!" Lance shrieked, jumping to his feet and rushing to the edge of the gorge, where he looked down at the painful sight of the smoldering chopper. "This can't be happening!"

Very slowly, Lance sank to one knee and buried his face in his hands. "I just found you, and now I've lost you again. How can this be?"

Lance felt a hand on his shoulder. Looking up, his eyes met
Jamie's. Rising to his feet, he pulled her tightly in his arms and held
her like he never wanted to let go. "Your dad told me the story,"
Jamie whispered in his ear. "He loved you very much, Lance."

"Why didn't he come to me sooner?" Lance pleaded. "Why did
he wait until now?"

Jamie moved a hand to the back of Lance's head and let her fingers
run through his raven hair. "Your dad was ashamed of what he had
done. He didn't know how you'd react when you discovered the truth."

"He lived his entire life alone, Jamie. And he died alone. It all
seems so unfair."

"He's not alone anymore," Jamie comforted. "He's finally where
he belongs, in your mother's arms."

Lance backed away a step. He took one more look at the remains
of the chopper, then turned back to Jamie. "I'm sorry," he told her. "I
had no right holding you like that. If Milton ever learned of it . . ."

"Milton has learned of it, Lance." At the sound of the unexpected
voice, Lance spun to see Milton, Charley, his grandfather, and Sheriff
Quinn all standing there looking on. In the commotion, Lance hadn't
even realized the second chopper had landed.

"Milton," Lance said, covering a cough with his fist. "I can
explain. It wasn't Jamie's fault . . ."

Milton stepped up to the two of them. "You have nothing to
explain, Lance. I'm a great detective, remember? I can deduce the truth
in most any situation all on my own. This one is easy." Lifting Jamie's
left hand, he very gently slipped off the ring. She didn't resist. "I won't
lie and say I didn't hope you'd stop me," he told her with a wink.

"I—I'm sorry, Milton."

"Don't be. This is for the best." He slid the ring into his pocket.
"Now," he said, wearing a genuine smile, "I think you two need at
least a little privacy to carry on whatever it was you were doing before
we walked up." He turned to the other men with him. "I realize you
have an investigation to do here, Quinn. But can't we start over there
by the culprit's Ranger? Surely you need to check out his vehicle to
see if there may be more evidence inside or something."

"Oh, yeah," Quinn said, obviously catching Milton's intention.
Stepping to the edge of the gorge, he glanced down at what was left

of the chopper. "Not much I can do about this, other than the 911 call I already made asking that the coroner be notified. I suppose we can start our investigation with the Ranger."

Milton took Quinn by the arm and led him off in the direction of the Ranger. Ivan and Charley held back momentarily. Ivan was the first to speak. "I guess you know I'm your grandfather, son," he humbly stated.

"Yes, Granddad, I know."

"And I guess you also know how grateful I am for you saving Jamie's life."

Through it all, Lance managed a smile. "I'm not sure she needed me all that much, Granddad. This lady knows how to handle herself. I think Jarvis would have been in trouble with or without Lance Gentry being on his tail."

"We both know that's not true, son," Ivan rebutted.

Jamie moved over to her father and kissed him on the cheek. "We all three know it's not true," she added. "I'm so sorry for the scare I gave you. You didn't deserve that."

Ivan pulled her into a brief hug, then turned his attention back to Lance. "We have a lot of catching up to do," he said. "That is, if it's all right with you."

"How soon can we start, Granddad?" he asked.

"The sooner the better, son."

The two men embraced, slapping each other on the back a few times, then Ivan pulled back nervously, glancing between Lance and Jamie. "If you two will excuse us, I think Quinn might need our help over at that Ranger. Come on, Charley, let's see what we can do."

"Wait!" Lance called. "Before you go, there's something I think you should know about the chopper pilot who saved our lives." Jamie shot a questioning look at Lance, but didn't interrupt. "You don't know this, Granddad, but Uncle Charley does. There's been an anonymous benefactor in my corner for several years now, helping with my education and the likes."

"The chopper pilot was that man?" Charley blurted out.

"Yeah. He just made his last, and his greatest, contribution."

"Who was he?" Charley pressed. "Did you learn his name before it was too late?"

"Yes, his name was . . ." Lance paused long enough to glance at Jamie, who still had that look on her face. "His name was Bart Madoc." Jamie drew a relieved breath and smiled. "Bart served in the war with my dad. He told me Dad died a real hero."

Charley nodded. "I always figured that, kid. I liked your dad. He was a great guy."

"Yes, he was," Lance agreed. "And so was Bart Madoc. I want that included on his gravestone. Bart Madoc, hero and a man greatly loved by all who knew him."

"I'll personally see to it, son," Ivan said. "The bill's on me."

"Thanks, Granddad. It means a lot."

Jamie slipped her arm through Lance's. "It means a lot to me too, Dad," she said.

Ivan straightened and took on a look of grave seriousness. "Do you know how confusing this is going to be?" he boldly stated. "Not knowing how to introduce this man? Will he be my grandson or my son-in-law?"

"Daddy!" Jamie shouted, her face beaming red.

"Come on, Charley," Ivan said. "Let's go help with that investigation."

CHAPTER 31

"It's been an eventful couple of days, hasn't it, Charley?" Lance remarked as they walked.

Charley laughed. "If you're looking for an argument on that point, you've come to the wrong guy."

Ivan stopped in his tracks when he noticed Allison had shown up from out of nowhere and was standing right in their path. "What's up?" Charley asked, realizing something had caused Ivan to stop. "Did you see a ghost?"

"Let me ask you a question," Ivan ventured. "Do you believe in ghosts? Or a better question would be, do you believe in angels?"

This brought a laugh. "Course I believe in ghosts and angels. I've played in plenty of movies on the subject."

"I'm not talking about movies, Charley. I'm talking the real thing. What would you say if I told you your sister is standing right in front of us at this very instant?"

"What are you doing?" Allison asked, a smile beaming on her face. "You know I can't show myself to Charley."

"Hey," Charley responded. "I have no problem with you telling me you feel Allison close by. What the heck, I've felt her close to me lots of times."

"No, Charley, you still don't understand what I'm saying. I don't just feel Allison next to me, I can see her standing right here, just as clearly as I can see you."

Charley raised an eyebrow. "You think you actually see her?" he quizzed.

"Allison," Ivan proposed. "Tell me something that no one could possibly know other than you and your brother here."

Her smile faded. "I'll have to think about that, Ivan," she remarked. "You've caught me a little off guard."

"Well, come up with something," he said. "I want Charley to know you're here, and that's the only way I can think to prove it."

Charley sobered. "Are you serious about this?" he asked. "Do you really believe Allison is here now?"

"Standing not two feet in front of you, Charley. I'm waiting for her to tell me something only you and she could know so I can prove it."

Charley rubbed his chin and retreated into deep thought. "There was a girl in the fifth grade. I fell madly in love with her, and Allison learned my secret."

"Brooke Stevens!" Allison half shouted. "She was a redhead, wore her hair in pigtails, and went by the nickname of Raisin."

Ivan's face broke into a cheerful grin. "Brooke Stevens," he said, taking great pleasure at seeing the look of astonishment on Charley's face. "A redhead who wore her hair in pigtails. She had a nickname, too. It was Raisin."

"Oh my gosh!" Charley gasped, eyes round and wide. "What did Raisin tell me when I asked her for a kiss?"

"She didn't tell you anything, Charley." Allison laughed with glee. "She jumped in and kissed you full on the mouth. Scared you so bad you ran off and never approached her again."

Ivan broke out laughing. "She kissed you and scared you off, Charley."

Charley laid a hand on Ivan's shoulder and leaned on him. "Allison?" he asked in disbelief. "Are you here?"

"Yes, Charley," Ivan responded soberly. "She is here. But I suspect she won't be sticking around much longer. Her work here is just about finished." Ivan looked to see Allison respond with a somber nod. "I thought so," he choked out. "But I wanted to give you and her the chance to feel each others' nearness before she leaves."

Allison was crying. "Thank you, Ivan. Tell Charley I love him and that I miss him more than words can say. And tell him thanks for doing such a great job raising our grandson."

"She loves you and misses you, Charley. And she says thanks for a job well-done raising Lance."

"Can—can she hear me?" Charley asked.

"Yes, she can hear you."

Charley swallowed. "I love you too, sis. And I want you to know, I think this guy you married is pretty great. It's taken awhile, but I've warmed up to him."

"Tell him . . ." Allison sobbed, ". . . that I said to get himself over there to that Pat Doyle and set things straight with her. It's time he had a woman in his life to settle him down. And I happen to know Pat is just the one who can do it."

Again Ivan laughed. "She's playing matchmaker, Charley. She wants you to hook up with that lady chopper pilot you seem to have known from someplace past. She says you need a woman in your life to help you settle down, and she knows this is the one who can do it."

"And tell him if she kisses him, to handle it better than he did with Raisin. No—wait!" she sniffled. "Don't tell him that. He's not a kid anymore. He's man enough now to figure that part out on his own."

Charley glanced over at the chopper where Pat was standing. "Do you think, sis?" he asked. "Is there a chance she'll take me back?"

"There's only one way to find out, Charley. Get over there and give it your best."

Ivan let his eyes roll between Allison and Charley. "She said yes," he fibbed. "The woman has it bad for you."

"Ivan!" Allison fussed. "That's not what I said! I don't know that for sure."

"I was in the chopper when you had your little exchange with her, Charley," Ivan went on, ignoring his wife's comment. "I can read a prospective jurist like I can read a newspaper. The jury won't be out long with this one. Go to her, Charley."

"That's what my sister told me to do?" he pressed.

"More or less."

"What?"

"Yes! That's what she said. Go to her, Charley."

"You'd better be right about this!" Allison scolded. "That's my brother's heart your playing with."

It was with all the confidence in the world that Ivan watched Charley walk away. "I'm right, Allison," he said. "I read it in her eyes. Can you hear their conversation, by chance?"

"I can do that, yes."

Ivan waited for Charley to reach Pat. "Okay," he said. "Tell me what they're saying."

"Charley's asking if there's any chance she might like to go out to dinner with him sometime," Allison responded.

"And what was her—" Ivan didn't get his question out, and didn't have to when he saw Pat throw her arms around Charley and plant a big kiss on his mouth. "Never mind, Allison, I think I know."

"Good for you, sweetheart," she laughed through her tears. "You amazed me with that one."

"Just like you amazed me with your prediction about Lance and Jamie."

"I had some extraterrestrial help on my end. You did yours on your own. I'm impressed."

"So, do you have any extraterrestrial help knowing about Milton's future?"

"Well I'll be, Ivan. You really care, don't you?"

"Milton's a good man. So how about it, does your angel status give you any vision into his future?"

"I don't suppose it'll hurt to tell you. There is someone special for Milton. She'll be crossing paths with him very soon now. The only reason I know this is the authorities told me for the same reason you asked. I was worried about him being hurt. I'll tell you who the lucky girl is if you swear to keep it to yourself. It's someone I'm sure you know of."

"My lips are sealed, I promise."

"Okay." She grinned. "Then I'll tell you. Sara Jefferson."

"Sara Jefferson? Isn't she? . . ."

"Ed Quinn's granddaughter."

"I'll be darned. Is that fitting, or is that fitting?" Ivan paused to look more deeply into his wife's eyes. "It's time, isn't it?" he forced himself to ask.

"Yes," she solemnly assured him. "It's time. There's just one more thing I need to do."

"And that is?" he asked.

"That trinket you keep on your key chain. It's time for it to go."

Ivan reached in his pocket and drew out his keys. "You mean this?" he asked, singling out the encapsulated bit of yellow ribbon taken from the crime scene where Rene was abducted.

Allison nodded. "That thing has been a symbol of your guilt for more years than I care to count, Ivan. It's time to get rid of it."

Ivan slipped the trinket off his chain. "You're right," he admitted. "I don't need this anymore." He turned and threw it through the barred window into the room he now knew had once held Rene captive. "That should be a good place for it," he remarked. "What happened in that room is all history now. It's a good place for that bit of ribbon to rot back to the dust where it originally came from."

"Yes, Ivan," she agreed. "It is a fitting place."

Ivan felt a tear trickle down his cheek. "I'm going to miss you, Allison. I'm going to miss you immensely."

"And I'll miss you, sweetheart. But just remember, when your time comes, I'll be there to meet you. Just like Rene was there for Neil."

Ivan look confused. "Rene greeted Neil? But how could that be since Neil died first?"

"Oh," Allison gasped, unable to hide her embarrassment. "I wasn't supposed to . . . That is, what I meant to say was . . . Oh, never mind. Just rest assured I will be the one to bring you home when your time is up."

"Any hint when that might be?" Ivan ventured.

"Not the slightest, other than to tell you—you will dance at your daughter's wedding. I'll be there too, but you'll have to trust me on that one." She brushed aside a tear. "It's my time, Ivan. I have to leave you now. My authorization is used up."

"Good-bye, Allison," he choked.

"Good-bye, my eternal sweetheart. See you soon."

Ivan closed his eyes as the bitterness of the moment bore down with excruciating pain. It was more than a minute before he could open them again. When he did, it was to see she was gone. "I love you, Allison!" he sobbed. "I'll always love you!"

I'll always love you too, my darling. Ivan heard the words, but only as a gentle voice from the innermost chambers of his heart. He turned to look at Lance and Jamie. As he did, he noticed something about himself. He was happier than he could ever remember being in his life. This self-forgiveness thing was pretty fantastic. Even better than winning the toughest court battle of the century.

CHAPTER 32

Jamie watched as her father and Charley walked away. Turning, she looked again into those dark, penetrating eyes. "So, where do we go from here?" she asked softly.

"You're sure about Milton?" Lance asked, unable to hide the hope from his voice.

Jamie felt the empty place on her finger. Milton was a fine man and one she had been almost certain she'd marry someday. But Milton never made her feel like she had those few moments she had been in Lance's arms. "I'm sure," she said, never lowering her eyes from his.

"Things went faster here than I supposed," he remarked. "I do have a job waiting back in Orlando."

"That's right, you do."

"I suppose there's nothing saying I can't extend my leave of absence, even though the original reason for it is finished."

She closed her eyes and felt her heart speed up. "You suppose?" she whispered.

"Let's just say I do extend it. And let's say I just happen to ask a certain young woman to spend some of that time with me? What do you think she might say back to me?"

Her eyes closed more tightly than ever, but even this didn't keep the tears from spilling. "I'm not sure I can answer that, Lance. Could you be more specific about what young woman you have in mind?"

He reached out and ran his fingers through her hair. "The one I have in mind is the daughter of a highly respected lawyer in these parts. She's a private investigator, one of the best I've ever come to know. And she's the most beautiful woman I've ever laid eyes on."

This was as far as Jamie could go with the little charade. Throwing herself in his arms, she pressed her lips to his and felt as if time had suddenly frozen on its course. The kiss lasted a very long time, and when it was over she pressed her wet face hard against his neck and felt warm, like a kitten cuddling to its mother. "Can I take that as a yes?" he asked. "Would she like to spend some time with me?"

"Only if you promise not to bug her for a DNA sample," she sobbed.

"Promise," he said. Then, pulling her face around, he kissed her again.

Somewhere off in the distance, she heard a familiar voice calling her name. Laying her head on Lance's shoulder again, she looked to see a most wonderful sight. There were three angels standing in front of the brightest light she had ever seen. Rene smiled and waved as she stood arm in arm with a most handsome man, a man who sported two good legs and showed not one sign of scarring. Jamie knew this was Neil. She also knew the third angel, although she wasn't sure how. This one was the mother who was waiting for her on the other side of forever. Very carefully, so as not to alert Lance, she raised a hand and returned the wave. The three of them smiled, then turned and walked into the light, which soon closed around them. And Jamie knew the man she was holding would be hers forever.

EPILOGUE

Lance and Jamie's wedding turned into a double wedding as they happily shared their day with Charley and Pat. At the reception, Ivan danced like he was a thirty-year-old man. But perhaps the happiest one in attendance was an unseen angel. An angel whose eyes had truly witnessed a dream come true.

ABOUT THE AUTHOR

"Writing has always been part of my life in one form or another," says Dan Yates. "Only now, in the shadow of my years, have I reached the pinnacle of fun that comes from spinning tales born of my own imagination. And yet, if I searched the depths of my imagination, I could never author a story to equal the one I've actually lived. I like to write about angels, and I've certainly had a few in my own pocket along the way."

A former bishop and high councilor, Dan lives with his wife, Shelby, in Phoenix, Arizona. They have six children and twenty grandchildren. Dan, who is now retired, spent several years of his career as a technical writer. He's also done several Church and local publications. His previous novels are: *Angels Don't Knock, Just Call Me an Angel, Angels to the Rescue, An Angel in the Family, It Takes an Angel, An Angel's Christmas, An Angel on Vacation,* and *An Angel in Time.* Dan loves hearing from his readers. He can be reached by e-mailing covenant-lds.com.